MENTION MY NAME IN HELL

BY
DANIEL
BOYD

MONTAG

First Montag Press E-Book and Paperback Original Edition September 2025

Montag Press ISBN: 978-1-957010-61-8
Design © 2025 Amit Dey

Montag Press Team:

Cover: Rick Febre
Author Photo: Helen Abston
Editor: Charlie Franco
Managing Director: Charlie Franco

A Montag Press Book
www.montagpress.com
Montag Press
777 Morton Street, Unit B
San Francisco CA 94129 USA

Montag Press, the burning book with the hatchet cover, the skewed word mark and the portrayal of the long-suffering fireman mascot are trademarks of Montag Press.

Printed & Digitally Originated in the United States of America
10 9 8 7 6 5 4 3 2 1

For Charlie
Who believed in me

PROLOGUE

"That's the problem with society today," Hinchley said, "People don't worry enough about the problems of the very rich."

His head bobbed strangely as he spoke, like the bust of a Greek orator wobbling on its pedestal. His hairy companion said nothing. They were studying a fine house in the distance and resting their horses at the edge of the woods, about fifty miles west of the town of Contention.

"You will observe, Mister Trask, that the estate before us is not a working ranch." Hinchley put a bony hand to his chin and squeezed his jaw between his fingers. The wobbling stopped. "It's an Estate. The property—I should say one small part of the property—of one Marcus Manderly. Well-kept and elaborate. Where a man of wealth can gather fine things about him and enjoy his success."

The squat, hairy man known as Slasher Jim Trask idly fingered the cutlass in his belt. It was his only weapon.

"You seem quite ready to use that pirate's toothpick, Mister Trask. Almost eager."

Trask didn't answer.

"But you know," Hinchley said, "When a man like Manderly has so much, there's always someone somewhere out there wanting to take it away from him. A pity, that."

"Yeah." Trask mounted his horse.

"Yes sir," Hinchley did likewise. "Just a pure shame."

They rode toward the house.

Seated comfortably in the well-appointed study inside his fine house, Marcus Manderly looked approvingly across the tea table at the dark-haired beauty sitting opposite him.

"... A peasant," she was saying, "A low-born half-*Yaqui* who claims noble birth because his servant-mother was seduced by her *Patron*. He believes he can erase his heritage by reading books. He deceives himself."

"But useful to us, eh?" Manderly glanced out the window as he spoke. Saw the two strangers riding across the well-kept lawn. Instinct warned him they meant him no good. He pulled a satin cord attached to a bell.

"He is the expert who will examine your Grimoire."

"And authenticate it?"

"I have only to put it properly to him."

A muscular butler entered.

"Yes Sir?"

"We have visitors, Bruno."

"I beg your pardon, Sir?"

"Visitors—" Manderly turned toward the window.

There was no one there.

Manderly pressed his face to the window, scanning from side to side.

No one in sight, and nothing to indicate there ever had been.

He shivered. "There-uh there may be something... There may be someone, I mean... there probably will be someone here. Soon."

"Yes Sir?"

"They want to talk to me. See that they don't."

"We shall, Sir. Will there be anything else?"

"Just be sure they're stopped. I don't like the look of them." Bruno looked out the window at nothing there.

"I'll see to it personally, Sir."

Manderly turned back to his guest. "I believe the Grimoire to be genuine. I just want to make certain he says so."

"Two months ago, he killed a man for me. I told him it was a question of my honor. If I put this to him properly, he will do as we wish."

"He'd better." Manderly put an edge to his words. "For your sake *Dona* Maria, he'd—" He turned as two men came into the room.

"I didn't think the boys could stop them," he sighed.

Dona Maria showed no sign of alarm.

"I'm Hinchley," The speaker was lean, well-spoken, and might have looked elegant if not for his oddly-set head. "This is Trask." He gestured politely toward his partner, who didn't look elegant at all. Never would. Never could.

"You know what we came for." Hinchley steadied his head again as he spoke.

"I do, and it's gone." Manderly curled his lips in a venomous grin with a gleam of triumph in it. "Sent where you'll never get your hands on it. Where even I can't reach it. On its way to Chicago, under Wells Fargo guard, accompanied by an expert, who will examine it in a carefully controlled setting, and then to New York, and then Rome, Italy."

"Pity," Hinchley mused aloud, "If you'd played this smarter, you could have lived a few seconds longer. But since you say even you can't get it…"

He turned to the lady.

"*Señora?* Will you do the honors?"

"With pleasure!" She turned to Manderly. Smiled pleasantly.

"Destroy yourself," she said.

CHAPTER 1

"Harvey?" I said, "You there?"

"Right here." The Devil was standing next to me at the bar, but I didn't turn to face him when he answered. Just kept my eyes on the drunk with the Navy Colt in his belt. I knew Harvey wouldn't mix into a fight, but I figured he might get me out of this one.

"Will you tell Gorsuch here to sober up and try me tomorrow?"

Harvey kept his voice respectful, which ain't easy when talking to a man like Christy Gorsuch. "Mister Gorsuch, you're picking a fight with Streak Wilson, and I know he's awful young yet, but he's really handy with firearms, and I suggest you sober up and try him tomorrow if you're still so inclined."

"Don't care." Gorsuch kept his hands well clear of his Colt, so maybe he wasn't as drunk as he looked.

"Well, live and learn," the Devil said. "Or die stupid if that suits you better."

I looked over at Christy Gorsuch to see if it changed his mind any.

It didn't. He gave Harvey a careful, drunken look. "I don't care if he's the best shot on green's God earth," He pointed at me. "That little sunuvabitch—" Set his empty shot glass on the bar and pointed at me again, so I'd know I'd been pointed at. "—He kilt my brother Buck. Old Buck that never hurt nobody. And fam'ly pride regulates that I must… uh…" He focused his eyes. Or maybe it was his mind. "Got to shoot him back for it, that's all. Kill'im."

He put one arm on the bar and stared at me straight on. "I wait your pressure inna street." His voice broke into a hiccup as he marched halfway through the swinging saloon doors, then paused and turned back to us with surprising grace.

"Take y'time." He executed a perfect About Face and marched off towards the general direction of outside.

I looked at the Devil. The Devil looked at me. Then for a while we just looked at Christy Gorsuch pacing up and down Commerce Street outside the Snake Ranch Saloon.

"What do you make of it, Streak?"

"Smells hinky as hell, Harvey—no offense to you."

"None at all. How did you like Mister Gorsuch's little show?"

"Still wondering what's best to do about it."

Harvey nodded and we both considered the thing for a while.

"I reckon most folks would just go out there and kill the little twit," Harvey said at last.

"What's a twit?"

"Sorry, Pard.'" The Devil toyed with his empty shot glass. Down the bar a little ways, underneath a twelve-foot rattlesnake which was dead, stuffed, and hung on the wall, Sam the bartender wiped the counter and sneaked a look at us, but kept his distance. Harvey bothers some folks that way, him being the Devil and all, but I've got used to it. "*Twit* is a word they use over in England to apply to men of no consequence. Like Christy Gorsuch, there."

"Guess it fits. He don't worry me none..." I had a near-beer on the bar in front of me, mostly untouched, because drinking near-beer ain't much to brag on. I stared at it and thought about other things. "He ain't near so drunk as he lets on, but he's a farmer, not a killer. No," I ran a finger around the rim of the glass. "No, I'm just considering on who put him up to this, and what else they might of thought up to do."

"That's worth considering, all right." Harvey looked out the door at Christy Gorsuch, still standing in the street and looking deadly as pink ribbons. Whilst he was watching, Justice Hopkins came in through the swinging doors, looked backwards over his shoulder at Christy, shook his head, and closed his black coat carefully over the badge pinned to his vest.

"Either of you gentlemen know what Gorsuch be doin' out there in the street? Like to scare the dogs away."

"Just getting himself ready to kill me is all."

"That so?" He signaled Sam for a drink. "Christy decide to buy the farm, did he?"

"He wants me to think so, anyhow."

"Here's to better days, Judge." Harvey raised his glass. "Young Streak and I are of the opinion he's not showing all his cards yet."

"Not playing with a full deck, more likely." Hopkins downed his drink and signaled for another. "You think someone put poor Christy up to this, do you?"

"I'm pretty close to thinking it. Only any man who wanted me dead would be a damn fool to give him the job."

Hopkins sipped his second drink slowly. "Wish we had time to give it proper thought."

"We'll make time for it. I don't care to go shooting first and figuring out afterwards, and I don't hardly think old Christy out there needs killing."

"Just what are you thinking on?"

"Back before I shot him, Christy's brother Buck used to ride with a man name of Pug Klavinsky. You recollect him?"

"Pug Klavinsky? Heavy-set man? Scarred wrists? Rides a dun mare?"

"That's the one."

"Never heard of him." Hopkins chuckled at his own joke and set down his glass. "But I did hear something as to how this Pug and his friends got a fondness for other men's horses and cattle."

"That's as may be. Big Bob Banneker got word as to how they lately got into the habit of stopping stagecoaches to make sure the horses ain't too heavy-loaded, and lifting the Fargo box to lighten 'em up some."

Hopkins nodded. "Seems I remember something along those lines. Ain't that how old Buck Gorsuch met his end? From being soft-hearted like that?"

Harvey grinned. "No, mostly from he took a shot at our friend Streak here, and missed."

I didn't like to think on that much, but there it was. A month back, two men tried to take the Red City stage and didn't make a very tall job of it. I killed one of them, and he turned out to be Buck Gorsuch. "I always figured it was Pug that high-tailed it off on a dun, but it was too far away for a shot, and that's too far to say for sure."

"A dun horse, you say?" Hopkins laid a nickel on the bar and took a cigar from a jar close by. "Wouldn't be the same as that dun mare racked down the street, would it?"

"I'd hate to bet on the difference." I collected up my long gun from where I'd leaned it against the bar.

He just nodded. Neither one of us had to call the play. Christy Gorsuch wasn't nearly the man to face me, and he wasn't figuring to. He was figuring on me facing him, whilst Pug Klavinsky drilled me in the back.

"I wonder how long it took old Pug to talk Christy around to it." Hopkins took a thoughtful puff on his stinkweed.

"And I wonder where Mister Klavinsky is waiting to take his shot from." Harvey finished his drink.

"And I wonder what the local lawman's going to do about all this." I sent a serious look straight at Hopkins.

It bounced right off.

"You got it wrong, sonny. All of it wrong. I'm the Justice here. Administrator of the Law. Not the Law itself. The good citizens of this fair blossom of the plains we call Contention aren't paying me near enough to handle that end of the business, and besides, they've got the wrong man anyway."

He went on like that, but I wasn't listening.

CHAPTER 2

I looked back out to the street.

Christy had backed up a ways north of the saloon door, so that when I came out I'd naturally turn to face him. That meant Pug would be holed up someplace close south of here. I got a picture in my mind of the street: Doc Lowell's… the Land Office… The Barber Shop, with its big glass window…

I tucked my long gun under one arm, "Reckon I'll go see about getting me a shave." And headed for the back door.

Out to the loading dock, and down the steps to the alley behind the shops on Commerce Street to the back of the Barber's.

Funny thing: I can't go into a Barber Shop without thinking how I first met Harvey in one. I guess they mostly all look alike, and sometimes I think all my troubles grew out of plush red chairs, perfumed oils, and old newspapers.

Come to think on it though, some good things grew out of that too, and I didn't have time for thinking anyhow. Soon as I walked in that back door, I spotted Pug Klavinsky watching the street, staring out the window with his back to me.

But not for long.

He spun around as soon as I entered, and stared. Stared across the room, past the revolving chair, the mirror and the shelf of fancy bottles, right into my eyes and then down to the .44 Spencer repeating rifle pointed at his belly.

He looked back up to my eyes again. "You hunting trouble, Wilson?"

That was old Pug, all right. Clear down to the dirt-caked toenails. Gets caught laying out an ambush, then turns right around and tries to load it on me.

"You got talent, Pug." I looked him straight in those deep-set sparkly eyes, eyes that shined with greed and get-more. "But that act would of worked better was you not holding that hog-leg."

He looked down at the Walker Colt in his right hand, like he'd never seen it before, and wasn't real well-acquainted with the hand, neither. I saved him the trouble of thinking up a lie and me the trouble of hearing it.

"Just set it down on the floor there. I ain't on no killing prod today."

Lately I'd heard myself talk like that—talk like killing a man was a thing I had a choice about. It bothered me some, but it worried Pug more. A man his age doesn't cotton much to taking orders from someone my age, but he minded the Spencer real good. Put his Colt down on the floor and showed his hands open and empty. "You got no call to pull iron on me, Wilson. I'm in here perfectly innocent."

I spoke to the Barber, but kept my eyes on Pug. "Is that a fact, Artie?"

"I don't know about perfect innocence. Can't think off-hand of anything Pug might be innocent of. All I can speak to is he needs a haircut, and hasn't asked for any barbering."

"He been chewing the breeze with the other loafers here?"

"No, nor batting the fat neither. Just came in here and begun to staring out the window."

I directed the conversation back to Pug. "Go on out and clean up the trash you dropped in the street."

"Hunh?"

"Christy Gorsuch. He's waiting out there to get my attention whilst you back-shoot me. Go clean that up. I'll follow behind to see you make a good job of it."

"Christy Gorsuch?" He gave me a look that I guess he thought was surprised or puzzled, or anything but guilty. "I never—"

"Do it, Pug." I saw his hackles go up, then lay back down again. He went out the door meek and quiet as a whipped dog, and I followed him.

Just two doors up, Christy Gorsuch was still standing in the middle of Commerce Street, folks were starting to notice, and it made him uncomfortable. He was staring at the saloon door, looking for me to come out, and wondering why I wasn't. I guess he was also looking for Pug to come out of the barber shop, but he sure wasn't looking to see him come out with me leading him from behind.

Funny how he took that. Just stood there blinking can't-believe-it, then got this ashamed look all over, like an actor that forgets his lines up on stage in front of everybody. He stared at us, not sure what to do next.

"Tell him to put down his gun, and you two ride out of here." I said.

It was a mistake. A bad mistake.

Pug called out to Christy all right, but what he said was, "The game's up, Christy. Save yourself while you can. He's gonna back-shoot me like he done to your brother Buck!"

And Christy took that as his signal to draw and fire.

CHAPTER 3

I knew better by now than to drink after a killing, so I sat in the Fargo office sipping strong coffee laced with honey whilst Big Bob Banneker sat across the room from me, filling out reports. All to once he turned his barrel belly around, looked at my face, and looked away again.

"Didn't I say you ain't to blame for it?"

"Yeah, you said that."

"Gorsuch fired twice at you."

"It was wild shots. Likely he would have emptied his gun and never hit me."

"Well, I sure hope you aren't dumb enough to think I'm dumb enough to hire me a guard dumb enough to take a chance like that. You figure you just ought to have stood there and let him try to kill you?"

He was right. And it didn't help a damn bit.

"I keep counting up the mistakes I made and seeing how I should have done it different."

"Mistakes like which?" He looked at his report. "I don't see any mistakes here."

"For one thing, Pug never much liked being called Pug. It's like he has this whole name that nobody ever calls him by it, nor uses it in front of him unless they hunger to get face-slapped or back-shot. But I said it there in the Barber's just to prod him up. And he got me back, right and proper."

"How's that?"

"I shouldn't of let him do the talking. Should of figured him for a sneak play like he done."

"Yes and he likely hoped you'd be the one to get shot. I sort of suspect Christy Gorsuch wasn't cheering you on, neither." Big Bob moved the papers to one side and took some time lighting up his pipe.

"I know you hate these." He handed me a cigar. "Atone for your sins with it."

Nothing on earth could have got a laugh out of me right then, nor even a smile. But that come close. I've heard of cigars making men sick, but Big Bob Banneker's are more like painful death. I lit mine anyway and drew in a deep lungful of harsh, bitter smoke tinged with a taste like spoiled meat. Big Bob stuck his pipe in his mouth and just kept it there whilst he talked.

"So you should have read Pug's mind, is that what you're telling me?"

"I should have... Hell, I just never figured he'd get his friend shot—not deliberate like that, anyhow."

"The only friend Pug has in this world or the next is the one he sees in a mirror. You didn't know that, and you're not to blame for not knowing it, because nobody ever told you.

Christy Gorsuch didn't have a snowball's chance of shooting you, but it was a chance, and Pug took it. I'm just surprised you didn't kill him, too."

"I come near close to it. He dived face-down in the street soon as Christy drew, and laid there saying his prayers till the shooting was over. Could have blowed his ugly head off, and I was sore tempted. Something about shooting an unarmed man in the back struck me wrong some ways."

"Well, he was sure setting up to do it to you."

"Whilst I was dealing with Christy Gorsuch, you mean."

"Always easier to back-shoot a man when he's got his mind on something else—like when he's stealing a horse, diddling your wife, or cheating at cards."

"I appreciate what you're trying to do, Bob, but I just ain't up for joking on it right now."

"So no one died except Christy-No-Account-Gorsuch, which was shooting at you, and you're all repentant over it?"

"Not just that, Bob. I don't clear understand it myself, maybe. But this here business of me killing folks has just naturally got to stop."

I stood up. "I'll maybe figure it out tonight. Or tomorrow. Till I do…" I took another drag of agony-smoke from the cigar. "Thanks for the poison, and good night."

CHAPTER 4

B ack in the Snake Ranch saloon, Sam the bartender poured bad whiskey into a smeary glass and passed it across the bar to Pug Klavinsky.

Pug downed it. Quickly. "Leave the bottle."

Sam took a careful look at him.

"That'll be a dollar."

"I ain't drunk a dollar's worth yet."

"Then I'll just keep this back here on the shelf till you do." He reached for the bottle and discovered Klavinsky's meaty hand in a death grip on the neck.

"The soldier stays here with me."

"Then gimme a dollar."

Klavinsky wavered. He had no desire to mix it up with the burly Sam. He did have a dollar, but that amounted to about a third or maybe a fourth of his total wealth—he wasn't good with figures—and he hated to spend it all in one place. But after a killing, he told himself, a man needs to get good and drunk. Falling-down drunk. So, the best thing would be...

CLINK!

His thoughts were interrupted by the sharp metallic ring of a Liberty Head five-dollar gold piece hitting the bar. Then a stranger's voice:

"Bring us a bottle of something better than this."

Klavinsky tried not to look surprised. Tried not to look obvious about it as he took careful stock of the stranger. Then tried not to look scared as his eyes went from the durable clothing flapping on his lean frame, up to the gaunt, oddly twisted face, and the wide leather collar that seemed to be holding his head on his shoulders.

Klavinsky looked away from it. The stranger spoke.

"The name is Hinchley." He poured a generous slug into Pug's glass.

"First name or last?"

"I'm not fussy." He gave the bartender a look that sent him down to the far end of the bar near a darkened corner where a short, hairy man sat waiting, his head barely above the counter.

"Klavinsky's mine."

"I know." Hinchley almost smiled. "That abbreviated gentleman at the end of the bar is my associate—" Hinchley nodded at the short man, and his head bobbed wildly for a moment. "James Trask."

Klavinsky glanced at the short man, square as a crate with long arms and a flattened head. Then he saw the cutlass hanging from his belt, and felt his stomach drop. "Jim Trask?"

"You've heard of him?"

"Not Slasher Jim Trask?"

"If you like. My friend's not choosy about names either." More liquor splashed into Klavinsky's glass and disappeared. "May we offer condolences on the death of your friend?" As he turned, his head twisted sideways—almost flopping around as he moved.

"Condolences is welcome," Klavinsky tossed the drink off. "And so's likker." He poured himself another and noticed his hands were shaking.

Hinchley noticed it too. "Drink to friends departed."

"I got other friends."

"So I'm told."

Pug drank, trying hard to ignore the way Hinchley's head seemed balanced on his shoulders rather than attached to them.

His host smiled. "You noticed my neck."

"What's wrong with it?"

"A few years back. During the War. I suffered a miscarriage of justice."

"Miscarriage, huh?"

"They hanged me."

Pug shivered.

"Occupational hazard in our line of work, eh?" Hinchley poured him another drink. "But enough of pleasantries. I have a use for a man with friends. Many of them. For something in your line of work, if I'm informed correctly."

"My line of work is anything that makes money," Klavinsky snorted. "What's the pay?"

"Five hundred dollars to start." The stranger looked pleased that Pug hadn't asked about the nature of the work. The sign of a true professional. "And another five hundred on completion. Plus expenses."

Pug looked pretty pleased himself, and a little less uncomfortable, but he tried to sound casual. "Expenses? What's this here expenses?"

"Your friends work for money, not love. And we may need a few men who share your -um- talents and experience."

"Guess I can round some up. Who we have to kill?"

"Have you ever heard of a Fargo agent named Streak Wilson?"

CHAPTER 5

I bunked upstairs in the Fargo office that night, but I didn't sleep much, thinking things through, about what was bothering me, and why it was. Then I went to figuring what to do about it, and after that, I didn't sleep at all. But I was feeling some better when I went downstairs for breakfast.

Big Bob Banneker always put out a morning feed for anyone at the office—drivers, clerks, passengers, or friends passing by. But the rest of them had mostly cleared out when I got there and filled a plate with biscuits and molasses.

"You got the look of a man with something to say." Big Bob set out a cup of hot coffee in front of me, then another one for himself.

"Guess it's a couple of things." I spread molasses on a biscuit. "One thing I'm wondering is how comes it I been working here two years and never got a run anywheres near Gunder's Station?"

He got kind of an awkward look on him. "You feeling homesick?"

"That ain't answering what I asked." I let him chew on that whilst I worked on a mouthful of biscuit till I could talk again.

"I guess I said plenty of times how I'd appreciate to get back there, and seems like you always put me on trips to hell-and-gone the other way."

"I got my reasons for it." He took a long drink of coffee whilst he come up with some. "For one thing, I need you on the high-value hauls. The ones that carry the big payloads. You've made a name for yourself. When word gets out you're riding shotgun, I can be damn sure the Fargo box on that stage is going to land where I pitched it at. For the last six months, nobody's tried—not even tried—anything vile on your runs."

"That would be the six months since I killed Buck Gorsuch, am I right, Bob?"

He just nodded.

"And that would make his brother Christy the eighth man in two years I've put in the ground for Fargo money."

For just a lick, I thought Big Bob was going to argue at me that shooting Christy was more of a personal matter than strictly Fargo business, and there's some men that would have, but Big Bob wasn't one to say his words in fine print, and he nodded again as to how we had to chalk Christy Gorsuch up to Fargo's account.

And then, just when I was all set to tell him that's why I was quitting, old Bob slipped a hook in me, so smooth and fast I never noticed till I was dangling on the line.

"What I'm saying, Streak, is… Oh Hell, you know Wells Fargo guarantees to deliver what we carry or else pay for it, so it just makes sense to put a man like you in between the road agents and the big money, don't you see? I got one coming up in the next few days—not sure yet what it is, but it must be something awful personal and important, I'm thinking."

"What you call a high-value load, huh?"

"Not just me. The fella that owned it killed himself three days after he shipped it out." He took a sip of coffee. "Rich man, he was, name of Manderly, shot his own self in the heart. And it ain't for sure, but I got an idea that cuss Klavinsky got wind of this shipment. And if he did, and if he wanted to grab for it, maybe he set up that little fracas with Christy just to make sure you wouldn't be the messenger on that run."

So that did it. I'd come in here full ready to quit this no-account job, and maybe Big Bob saw that, or maybe not, but he'd got me hooked back to him, and he knew it. Bad as I felt about Christy Gorsuch dead, I felt even badder about Pug Klavinsky alive. And I might could put a stop to that if I kept on riding for Fargo and Banneker.

I made one last try to unhook myself. "Don't you never send anything valuable to Gunder's Station?"

"Fact is, hardly ever. And getting hardlyer all the time. Don't even run a steady stage line to Gunder's Station no more."

I must have looked pretty surprised right then, because Big Bob went on without me asking.

"That town ain't been the same since you–" He started to say something, then reined back and put it different. "—since Boxapple Ranch folded up. Some Eastern concern owns it now, sitting on the land till they make up their minds what to do with it. Most folks there, well, they've pulled up stakes and emigrated themselves elsewhere. Business moved on with 'em and so did we."

Right away I got to thinking on Frenchy's Barber Shop and Deakins' Dry Goods, but mostly about Sally Gal and her little place. "I never heard about any of that."

"No need you should. It ain't news when a town dies. It happens so slow and so quiet, most folks don't even see it coming on till it's gone plumb off. I wouldn't have noticed it myself, only it's my work to keep track of business like that."

"Well then, maybe you reckon you could send me along next time a stage does go that ways?"

"I could." He emptied his cup down his mouth. "But I'm not gonna."

"You got a good reason?"

"Good enough. Was you to go anywhere near Gunder's Station now, there's them'd see you hang."

"Come again?"

"There's talk there against you. Lots of talk, all of it concerned around the untimely demise of the whole Appley family and how the Boxapple Ranch went out of business right about then. Bad times has hit these folks hard, and some of 'em says you're to blame."

"Just how do you figure that?"

"I don't. It ain't me that says it. Me, I know Boxapple was losing money pretty hard. Had been for years, but it all fell apart when old Man Appley and his boy Junior Jim departed… like they did."

"That wasn't none of my doing."

"Talk has it you were right close by and handy."

"Lots of folks was."

"Both times."

"I couldn't help that."

"No, you couldn't help being where you were, and that's the sad truth of it. But truth don't enter into this here talk about you. And talk can kill a man like… Hell, I even heard someone sermonize about how you shot Appley when he was too crippled up to draw on you."

"There's them as knows better."

"A while ago back there was. Before Frenchy took his family and set up shop in Greenville. Jim Deakins sold out too, and I don't even know where he went."

"There was plenty of Box Apple hands…"

"And they hit the grub line when Boxapple folded." He took out his pipe and filled the room with smoke. Maybe that's what made my eyes water. "Streak, you're a good man, and looked on with a fair amount of favor hereabouts. But in Gunder's Station, your friends are hard to find, except for--"

I knew what he was going to say next, so I just waited for him to get on with it.

"And that's another thing: That fella you ride with… What's his name?"

"Harvey Rideout, you mean?"

"He's low company."

"Ain't such a bad sort once you get to knowing him."

"He rubs folks wrong."

"Some folks."

"My dog come near to bitin' him."

"Some animals he rubs wrong, too."

"There's even them that call him the Devil."

"You believe them?"

"I do not." He poked his pipe stem at me. "And I'll thank you not to put me in a class marked by ignorant superstition. But the fact remains, there's just something about him that unsettles a man. Something pure evil. And you ride with him."

I had to admit to myself, Big Bob was right. But I didn't have to admit it to him.

"We get along okay."

"You do. And it worries me."

"Well, stop your worrying." I stood up.

"Sit back down." Big Bob waved his pipe again. "You said there was two things bothering your mind."

"Not anymore."

"You're sticking with me, now? With Fargo?"

"At least till this next job gets done."

"I got your word on that?"

"I said it."

"Good enough for me. That next run goes out in about ten days. Make it Friday. So—" He stirred the tobacco in his pipe with a matchstick, then struck the match on his thumb and re-lighted it. "How keen are you to put the quietus on Pug Klavinsky, Streak?"

"Keen enough to wait till you get around to telling me whatever you got in mind, I guess."

Big Bob grinned at that. "Well, you just take yourself a nice long ride anyplace and don't show up here again till Friday morning early. In fact, don't show here at all. You can meet the stage at the East Fork swing station. I'll spread talk as to how you quit Fargo and moved on." He grinned. "And like I say: Talk can kill a man."

Outside, I looked up and down the street, scanning for anything unfriendly, which was another bad habit I got from two years doing this work. Pug Klavinsky was across the street, loafing outside the saloon, sitting back on a bench with his hat down just enough to shadow his eyes so I couldn't see what he was looking at.

But I could guess it pretty good.

CHAPTER 6

"**Y**ou're here."

Hinchley held the door for Pug Klavinsky. As he moved, his head wobbled above the wide leather collar, and for a moment Pug expected it to fall off and roll onto the floor. He turned away from the sight, made himself look around the sparsely furnished hotel room, past the squat, hairy figure of Slasher Jim Trask lying naked on the bed, and he wished his host had set this meeting for the Snake Ranch.

"You got my message?"

"You said you need money." Hinchley didn't look glad about it. Or upset, either. "I was expecting it." He raised a hand to his chin and used it to move his head till he faced Klavinsky. "How much and what for?"

Klavinsky took a quick glance at Trask, whose eyes seemed to be watching him with quiet intensity from somewhere deep and dark, between bushy eyebrows and tangled beard, like a wolf peering through the underbrush. Pug cleared his throat. "Two Hundred. To pay our respects to Wilson."

"That's a lot of money for one man."

"I got a lot of friends. I want more than one of 'em for this job."

"I'm not sure we need them. I heard Wilson quit Fargo and left town."

"You believe it?" Klavinsky tried to focus on anything in the room but the two men who shared it. Nothing worked.

"Should I not?"

"Not if this job is so almighty important like you say it is."

From the bed, Slasher Jim made a noise that might have been a snort or a soft growl.

Hinchley regarded Klavinsky closely. "Moreso than I can say or you would believe."

"You sure act like it." Klavinsky looked over to the bed as another feral noise came from Slasher Jim. He turned back to Hinchley, then cast a sidelong glance back at Trask. There was something about the two men together...

"So, if we assume that Wilson hasn't left?" His host prompted.

"He's left town, okay. I just ain't sure if he's left off working for Fargo."

"I take it you expect him to be on next week's run."

"I'd look for him to be here first thing Friday morning, ready to follow the stage. Unless I round up some of the boys and set 'em to paying him a social call."

Hinchley drew a fat wallet from inside his coat "You know where he is?" He fanned out a few large bills and passed them to Pug.

"Not for sure." Pug reached out—carefully avoiding direct touch of the hands—and pocketed the money with the practiced grace of a coyote on a carcass. "But I got me a pretty good idea where he's going."

"Then see that he's put out of our way." Hinchley rose and moved to the door in a way that somehow seemed to sweep Klavinsky out of the room. "This is essential."

Out in the hallway before he knew it, Klavinsky tucked the money securely in his pocket and turned to ask the question that bothered him.

"If you're so almighty concerned about beefin' Streak Wilson, and you got Slasher Jim Trask right there in the room with ya, why don't you just set him on the scent? Come to that, I don't see why you invited me to this-hear dance at all." He made himself look directly at Hinchley.

But his host was gone. The door was closed.

And Klavinsky had the odd feeling that the room he had just left was now empty.

CHAPTER 7

We'd been on the road since yesterday, me and the Devil. Didn't need any map to get where I was headed, because I was going nowhere, and I knew the way by heart.

"What was the other thing, anyway?" Harvey asked. "The thing you never got around to telling Banneker?"

"This feeling like I kill folks for money."

"It's what you do, you know. What about it?"

"I'm getting too much used to it. So it comes easy and don't bother me. I don't like that. Don't like it at all."

Harvey didn't say anything to that, so we just rode for a ways, him on the Tennessee Stud, and me on Bucky, who's getting a little age on him now, but still the smartest cow pony I ever met.

And after a time, Harvey comes out with, "Not sure I follow you real close, Streak. Are you saying it bothers you because it doesn't bother you?"

"Big Bob Banneker and the Fargo Company call me a Messenger, and they say I'm paid to guard property, but when you come down to it, I just kill men for the sake of money. That's all it is."

"Hmmmm," Harvey mulled that in his mind. "Best remember, those men you plant in the ground are full-on ready to kill you too, for the sake of that money."

"That's the only thing that eases my mind—that and I didn't know any better when I got into this line of work."

"And now you tumbled to it, you're getting out."

"Soon as I settle old Pug."

"One last job, and that's all, eh?"

"I sure don't aim to make a living this-a-ways."

"You'd be surprised how many do, one way and another. And how easy it gets to be. Hard to give up, too."

"Not for me."

"You know another trade, do you?"

"Hunh?"

"What I mean is, you don't do you?"

"Don't what?"

"You don't know another trade. You've never farmed, can't afford a ranch, don't know prospecting, lumber-jacking, milling, mining, bartending, faro-dealing, store-clerking…"

"I get the idea, Harve. And I'll be just as happy to take up starving for a living if I got to."

"Well, I hope it turns out you're right. And if you're not right, I hope you don't hurt yourself too bad finding it out."

I thought that one over. Then, "Don't you know? Can't you see into the future?"

"I can. Don't. Not much point in it, really. I find if I stay where I am long enough, the future catches up with me sooner or later."

"Okay, you got your reasons, as far as they go. But for folks like me… Just seems like a man could better himself considerable, knowing what was to come."

"He could, but nine times to a dozen he won't."

"How's that?"

"Some folks call it free will. Others say it's just plain cussedness. Comes down to how a man climbs his own hill." He got a thoughtful look on his face. "Let's say what if I was to look into the future, see you're headed to ruination, and tell you to change your ways?"

"Seems to me you did that once, and I wouldn't listen."

"I recall the unhappy consequences of it all too well. But let's suppose you'd decide to change course and avoid the grief." Harvey patted Tennessee's mane with a gentle hand. "Only what direction do you go? And how do you get there?"

He pulled the reins left to steer his horse away from a rabbit hole, then a sharp right to keep from hitting a low-hanging branch, as the trail turned hilly and started climbing.

"See? It's like that. If you'd listened to me and dodged that sorrow, you would have changed the future. Opened up a whole raft of possibilities, some good, some a whole lot worse than what came out of you not listening to me." He shook his head like a man carrying a load of regret. "You don't get to change just one thing. Not ever."

"I think I see what you're saying, Harvey."

"Then just forget it, friend. Mostly nobody listens any more than you did."

"They don't?" Bucky was breathing heavy with the climb, so I slowed him up some.

"They do not."

"How come?"

"I couldn't say. Maybe because the wicked are so damn stupid, and the righteous think they know better. Comes down to the same thing."

I pondered over which kind of fool I was, and after a time that sad excuse for a road finally reached the crest of the hill and opened out onto a clearing, and I was looking down the other side on old Black Ben's shack.

Not that I could have missed it.

Most men who live in shacks don't care much how the place looks. Black Ben cared, but he cared crazy. He'd got some paint and covered the place with it. Actually, he'd got a lot of paint somewhere, but never enough of any one color. One wall was blue. Or mostly blue, except the bottom two feet of it was painted turquoise. Another wall was part red and part purple, and the next was orange and black. The front was all green—except for the porch, which was the brightest yellow I ever saw.

I just sat there on Bucky and looked at it for a while. It was a place that deserved looking at.

"I can't make up my mind if it's crazy-ugly or if it's pretty in its own way." I looked at Harvey to see how it took him.

"Or maybe kind of funny." He offered.

"Like old Ben might have painted it that way for a joke?"

"Old Ben?"

"Folks call him Black Ben. Plays his fiddle at parties and church socials and the like."

"I seem to recall the gentleman."

"That's him stepping out on the porch."

"That nasty-eyed fellow with the firearm?"

""You guessed it, Harvey."

"You suppose he means to use it?"

"He'd rather hang me, from the look of him."

"Well, seeing as how you don't want to owe me any favors…"

He was gone. Him and Tennessee both. And Black Ben was pointing a big old Navy Colt my way.

I just sighed, "Welcome back to Gunder's Station, Mister Wilson." and headed Bucky down the gentle slope to Black Ben's crazy house.

CHAPTER 8

One thing I learned in two years riding the Fargo Box: When a man points a gun at you but don't shoot right away, it's because he doesn't really want to. Ben hadn't, so he most likely didn't. And I knew for certain I wasn't near to shooting him, so I wasn't real fretful about the situation.

But Lawsy! Black Ben had a hateful look on his face.

"Ben," I said, "You sure got a baleful stare."

"Whut's baleful?"

"It's a word I read last week. '*He fixed him with a baleful stare.*' It means pure unfriendly-like."

"Well, that's truth. I never had no use for you anyhow, and now why you come bringing the Devil right up to my door?"

"You knew that was Harv—the devil?"

"We've met. And what he done, I never want to see him do it again. "

"Maybe you just never got to know him."

"Don't joke on it." He pointed the Navy Colt at my face for emphasis. "Don't you never joke about goin' to Hell, 'cause you surely heading there."

"I'm sorry, Ben." I most generally try to step light around another man's religion, and this seemed like a real good time to keep in practice.

"Gonna be a whole lot sorrier, come the judgement day." He lowered the gun. "Now what you want with me, anyhow?"

"I'm just wondering." I wanted to dismount and talk closer up, but the look on Black Ben's face said my feet weren't welcome on his ground. "About Gunder's Station and about… about everybody there."

Something gentled down on his face. When he spoke, his voice was almost friendly.

"Seems like more'n a year ago since you left off riding these-here hills."

"Two years, more like."

He gave me a searching look. "Reckon you're wondering what become of that Jezebel you used to consort with."

"I'd like to know," I gave him his look back and added a little something of my own to go with it. "But I won't hear you talk about her with those words, nor anything like 'em."

His jaw set and his shoulders went back, ready for a fight I didn't want to start. "I'm not making a threat, Ben. I'm just saying it, and I'll ask you to respect it."

"Fair enough," he nodded. "That Sally Gal moved on."

"When?"

"Not long back. A month, maybe less."

"Where to?"

"White folks don't tell me all they planning."

"Any idea who might know?"

"Fella bought her place out might have him a notion."

It made sense. But "I heard it ain't real safe for me in Gunder's Station."

"Most of my life, folks been telling me places I ain't supposed to go." He almost grinned, then remembered it was his Christian duty to hate me. "Never made much difference to me."

"I'm obliged, Ben."

"I'm thinking back how you done me a kindness one time and another, now you be paid back."

"Suits me."

"So if I do you another good turn, you owes me one back, don'cha?"

"I guess so, if you see it that way. I just figure when you do something for a friend, you don't look for—"

"We ain't friends and never gonna be."

"I see it different."

"And how come that?"

"Because I like you."

"Well, you just quit doing that. Stop it, y'hear? That's the favor I aim to get from you."

"You call that a favor?"

"You heard me. I'm readied up to do you a good thing, and once I do that, you pay me back by not barging in here no more ever. And should you do come calling, you come calling set to do some fancy shooting, 'cause I don't aim to let you get that first shot."

"I hear you Ben, I just don't reckon you'd kill me on sight."

"You show your face here again and see if I don't."

"Then what's this favor you're going to do for me?"

"It's a telling favor. I'm gonna tell you something worth the knowing."

"And what's that?"

"First, I got your promise, you don't come around here no more. Not ever. Lest I shoot you. Shoot you down. You promise, white trash?"

"I promise you, Ben."

"Okay, here 'tis: That Sally Gal. She quit town."

"You told me that already."

"Purely had to do it and get it done fast. On account of she killed a man."

"How's that?"

"You heard me right, I reckon."

I tried to think it through. I've seen Sally Gal riled up, and no, I wouldn't expect her to kill a man.

But it wouldn't surprise me much, neither.

"Is the Law after her?"

He snorted. "Ain't had proper Law in this place ever. Never needed it. She didn't miss it done herself." He shook his head. "Your Sally Gal got herself in a fight with some drunken cowboy. He come at her with a broken bottle and she struck him clear dead with a bung hammer."

"There was plenty of witnesses, then?"

"There was. Only she figured it be wise to vacate anyhow."

And she'd be right. I thought back on what Big Bob Banneker said about the stories they told about me and the night old man Appley died. And yeah, I could see as how relocating was the safe and smart thing.

"And you don't know where she's gone to?"

"I told you it once, didn't I?"

"Well, that's some favor you done me, Ben."

"You just hold up your side of the deal, and I don't get your killin' on my conscience."

I didn't answer. Just reined Bucky around and rode away. Didn't say my thank yous nor goodbyes, nor nothing like that. I was too much worried over what Black Ben said, so bad I could only think one thing.

Sally Gal needed me.

CHAPTER 9

We'd been on the trail toward Gunder's Station for maybe half an hour before the Devil asked me, "You looking to find that woman?"

"As questions go, that ain't much of one, Harvey. Reckon we both know why I'm headed this way."

"Back to Gunder's Station?"

"Likely somebody there knows where she's gone to."

"You're not exactly the fair-haired boy around there these days."

"So I hear."

"Might get a cold reception from the locals—or worse yet, a hot one."

"Maybe I will. Maybe I think it's worth the trouble."

"There's easier ways to find her, you know."

"Like asking you?"

"And why not? I'll give you this one free of obligation."

"Harvey, I like you." I reined up to face him. "You're fine company, and you've always been square with me. So I hope you don't take offense if I say... Hell, I just got through swapping favors with a fella. Didn't like it much. And I'd rather not owe you any."

He chewed on that for a time. "You always were an independent cuss, Streak." He gave the reins a gentle tug to get his animal moving again.

After a while he added, "Stubborn, too."

And a long time beyond that, he threw in, "I kind of like that about you."

By then we'd got to Gunder's Station, and I seen Big Bob Banneker was right.

It was a town busy at dying on its feet.

"Seems like Deakins' Dry Goods used to set over there. And the nice house Jim Deakins built for his family." I wheeled Bucky that way.

"Not anymore," Harvey shook his head. "Both been torn down for wood. Same with Frenchy's old barber shop and the house where his baby got born, that night when … you had to leave town."

It hit me kind of hard. "Likely the four best buildings in Gunder's Station, and now they're clear gone?"

"Gone as wildflowers in winter."

"I see Bart Gunder's livery's still standing. Anyhow it was always the biggest building hereabouts."

"The oldest, too," Harvey said. "Way I heard it, Bart Gunder used to have him a farm right here on the road a day's ride north of Contention—that's a fair-sized town, y'know—and just about as far south of Scogginsville, which is likewise. So he turned his barn into a livery and fitted the loft up into sleeping quarters, and he named the whole works Gunder's Station, even if it was just a barn and a corral."

So that was how the town of Gunder's Station got started, and it looked fair likely to end up that way too. The barn could have stood still for some fresh paint, and I could smell it needed a good cleaning, even from a long ways off.

"Wonder if there's anyone here as might be glad to see me?"

"You could light down there and find out," Harvey shrugged, "If you figure there's no hurry over that Sally Gal on your mind."

He was right. Instead of hitching at the rail, I'd been going right past Sally Gal's old place to Gunder's livery, reason being I was afraid of what I might find out—or not.

"Thanks." I pulled Bucky up and over to the faded-white little building where I first saw Sally Gal, and where I last saw her, selling liquor to cowboys who nursed drinks to spend time with her.

"I'll trickle on down to the livery myself." Harvey nodded and headed off.

Inside, Sally Gal's place was… I don't know how to say it. The same but different. The new owner—likely the skinny, pinch-faced man standing behind the bar, talking down to an even scrawnier copper-haired girl, barefoot in a feedsack dress and a long dirty apron—this guy hadn't washed down the walls, like Sally Gal used to, nor wiped the windows, nor… Well come down to it, he hadn't actually changed anything, he just hadn't took care of it, neither.

There were maybe a half-dozen men in there, counting me and the barkeep. Two of them were sitting at a table in the corner, dealing cards to each other, and they looked me over kind of close, like maybe they thought I'd walk up and ask to sit in.

The rest of the crowd—two cowboys—was slumped half-across the bar, fingering empty glasses and eyeing me up same as the gamblers. I made to ignore them, waited for the bartender to finish with the girl and send her out the back door. Tried to shake the feeling I was getting watched and watched hard by somebody who'd like to see me dead. Made me kind of wish Harvey'd come in with me, so's I could ask him if Hell was any worse place than this here.

I didn't see how it could be.

The copper-haired girl went out the back way, and a few minutes later come back in, almost. She was trying to shove a barrel through the door and not finding much success in the enterprise, the barrel being too tall to roll sideways and too heavy for her to move other than by backing up and slamming her shoulder against it.

I stood at the bar and ran a finger along it, across a scuffed place which I'd made years back, jumping over the top to kiss Sally Gal. Just remembering it made me feel all over funny, glad to see it and remember things a little. Then I got to thinking how Sally could have sanded that mark down and erased it, but she hadn't done that. Maybe she just didn't notice, or maybe…

"What's it be, Mister?" The Barkeep gave me a trace of smile out of his gap-toothed mouth, and I said I'd have a near-beer for starters. "But I'm not hurrying. Go ahead and give your little girl a hand with that barrel, if you've a mind to."

He didn't answer. Just served me up a thick-bottomed glass full of something warm and yellow-brown. I sipped it, decided that was plenty, thank you, and looked around while he just stood behind the bar, and never said a word to me nor stirred to help that little girl.

I guess it don't take much to get my fill of that. I set down my excuse for a drink and headed to the back door, where that girl had got herself and the barrel both good and stuck. I reached down, pulled her clear, then grabbed the barrel by the top and pulled it inside. Tipped it over so's she could roll it to wherever.

I turned back to the barkeep. "You own this place now?" Something told me to act like it wasn't important one way or another.

"Yup." He wiped a glass, looking morose. That's another word I learned from reading in books: *morose*. It means sad and regretful. Maybe he was ashamed of how he treated that girl, or it might have been the weak, warm beer that got him all morose.

"What happened to the Lady as used to own it?"

"She got ugly."

"What you mean, *she got ugly*??"

"I mean she got ugly. Her face got ruined. Some man tried to beat her up, and when he couldn't whup her, he broke a bottle on her face. Scarred her up so bad folks stopped coming in her place for a drink, on account of they didn't wanna look at her, she was that ugly. You don't want no business with her now."

"Where'd she go?"

"Can't say."

"Not even for cash money?"

"Listen, drifter," He sighed, left off wiping dust out of glasses, and looked me straight on. "I'd as soon you didn't go throwing temptation at me, 'cause I can't duck or dodge real good. Never could. And this lady—I'll say she's a lady, even if she did run a saloon—she told me where she was going, and she told me to keep it to myself, as a favor to her, and she looked so bad right then..."

"And I'll say that was one ugly woman."

One of the cowboys at the end of the bar said that. Said it kind of loud, like he wanted to be sure I heard it.

Across the room, the gamblers put away their cards.

"Say it?" The other cowboy echoed, "I'll carve it on a tree!" He sort of half-stepped away from the bar, moving toward me relaxed and harmless-like, and his right hand just naturally went down to rest at his belt.

"Hurt my eyes just to—" He squinted at my head and broke off sudden. "Say, ain't you the kid they used to call Streak Wilson?"

He was looking right at the streak of white in my hair, which I brought back from the War. And I didn't like it much. Didn't like how they were talking about Sally Gal deliberate so's I could hear it, and I never much cared to be called a kid, even if I am still shy of twenty by a few years. Seemed like I'd had my share and then some, carrying that name—Kid—and it bothered me more every time I heard it.

But mostly I didn't like the feeling in the room, the excitement on the faces of just about everybody there, that they were going to see a good fight or else make one. I'd felt it plenty before and

"I'm getting tired of it," I said.

"Tired of what?"

So maybe I wasn't kindly disposed, and maybe I should have remembered I was in here trying to find out about Sally Gal, not start a fight. But maybe don't count for much in this world or the next.

Still, I tried. "Nothing, never mind." I turned back to the bartender. "So what become of that woman that owned—"

It didn't work. The loud cowboy took a step closer my way. I turned back to him, slowly, hands low and wide.

"But I ain't askin' now." Close-up, his breath was sour with booze, but he didn't move like a drunk, nor talk like one, either. Come to that, he wasn't deep-tanned the way cowboys get.

"You're Streak Wilson." He said it to the room in general, and the two gamblers sat up and took notice. "The killer that shot down poor old Jim Appley right across the street from here. And I'm calling you a yellow coward for what you done."

I gave him a quick once-over without moving my eyes from his. Took stock of the polished grip on the six-gun stowed in his belt, the shiny-handled knife in his boot, and cold murder in his steady glare. The men at the card table watched closer now, and the barefoot girl stopped scuffing that barrel across the floor. So the cowboy must have decided he'd give'em something worth taking a look at.

They did, but it didn't last long. I moved my right hand down to the Smith Revolver on my hip—it looked like I was going to need it—and the cowboy's left came out to block my draw, fast like he'd had some practice. I grabbed the beer mug off the bar with my own left and swung it at his head, but he ducked down, pulled the knife out of his boot and widened his stance for a quick thrust up my innards.

Which was when I took a step back out of danger and kicked his knee apart.

He screamed. Loud.

I pulled the Smith while he was busy falling, leveled it at the room in general, checked to see that nobody'd got behind me. The bartender had a heavy mallet in his hand, like they tap beer barrels with, but he didn't seem real anxious to use it.

I looked around the room again. The girl was hiding behind the barrel and looking like she wished she could get inside it.

"Is this over with? Or does anybody else here figure they owe me some trouble?"

For a few long seconds, the only sound was from the cowboy on the floor holding his broken knee and grinding his teeth to keep from screaming. Then,

"It's over," the Bardog grunted. "But I want you gone."

"I'll git," I scanned the room again. "But first tell me—"

One of the card players in the far corner pulled a double-barrel shotgun out from under the table.

"Damn!"

I spent half a split-second hoping it wouldn't happen. Then wishing it didn't. Then it did. He swung the muzzle my way and got his finger on the triggers.

The girl tipped the barrel on its side and sent it rolling his way.

I already said how years back, I jumped over that bar just in a hurry to be with Sally Gal. Maybe that's what saved my life, knowing I could do it easy. Anyhow, I went over fast, hit the floor thankful, and crouched down low. Somewhere in between, I heard the dead-loud roar of twin smooth-bores spitting buckshot. The barkeep, blown back by a blast of lead, smacked the wall, folded at the knees, and sat down on the floor right next to me with his dead eyes open and that big mallet still tight in his fist.

There was a time when that would've slowed me up, but that time wasn't now. I wasn't even aware of coming up with my gun pointed into the corner and sending a round into the unlucky card-player holding the empty shotgun that just killed the wrong man.

It was over before I even knew it was going to happen.

CHAPTER 10

There was empty and there was quiet. Down at my feet behind the bar, a dead man sat on the floor, his mouth open and eyes staring blind. In front, the cowboy I kicked had quit complaining over the pain in his knee—that charge of buckshot meant for me had done for him and the barkeep both. His drinking buddy had beat the other card-player out the back door, but not by much.

I was alone in Sally Gal's place with three dead men.

No, not alone; that barrel-rolling girl was curled up in a tiny ball in the middle of the floor.

First things needed doing first. I took a good look at the dead cowboy to see for certain he was dead, and he surely was. Also, I'd never seen him before, so he wasn't from around here.

I bent down to check on the girl. "Missy? You okay?" She uncurled slow-like, feeling along her arms and legs as they straightened. "You didn't get hit, didja?"

"Naah." I expected she'd be shook up, crying, maybe screaming even, but she just shook it off. Stood and looked me up-down-and-sideways. "You got the way about you."

I was already across the room for a squint down at the dead gambler. His dark coat was dirty and worn at the elbows, and he needed a shave. Hard telling about his shirt, bloody from the hole in his chest, but it didn't look too new nor very clean. I studied his face, but couldn't think if I'd ever seen him before. Not here in Gunder's Station, that was sure.

So there it was. Neither one of them lived around here back when I did. One stranger had tried to start a fight so's he could pull a knife on me. Another tried to kill me outright. I wondered about the why of it.

"You handled 'em both," the girl said, "They was laying for you, but you got both of 'em and scared the rest away."

"Maybe, but not real far away." Outside, the other two had made their way to the street in front and begun to making a lot of noise over the situation.

"It's Wilson! He's come back a-killing!"

"Two men dead in there!"

"No-three! Wasn't even in there five minutes and killed three men!"

"Just walked in and started shooting…"

Oh Hell.

I turned to the Girl. "What do they call you at home?"

"Call me Kelly. My Pappy called me Wilhelmina when he give me a beatin' but mostly I'm called Kelly."

"You saw what happened, Kelly?"

"I surely did, Sir. They was laying for you but—"

"How long they been in town here?"

"Just about a day or two."

"Them two outside. Did you catch their names?"

"The one with the cards, they called him Fingers. Just Fingers. And the cowboy, I'm not sure, but I think it was Brownie Something."

I called to mind an old Fargo notice. "Was it Brownie Davis, maybe?"

"Could be, Sir. Ain't for certain."

"And the other one, you recollect, did they call him Finnegan?"

"Could be they did. I kind of think I remember it, but I ain't for sure."

"You just don't go away then." Nothing else for it. I opened the Smith and plucked out the spent shell. Put in a fresh cartridge and walked outside.

The two men stopped yapping real sudden, but they'd drawn a crowd. I felt a dozen or so pairs of eyes on me, and quiet hate like a strong wind in my face. I kept my voice steady and talked loud enough to be heard, but not yelling.

"There's your bartender and a cowboy dead from a shotgun in there. I killed the man that killed them." I tossed the shell casing on the boardwalk in front of everyone. "That's the spent cartridge from the only shot I fired. Go look, you'll see the man I killed—him and his scatter-gun over in the far corner from where I was." I looked around at the hostile faces. "Kelly, in there, saw it happen. I figure most of you can see the difference between a dead man pistol-shot, and two that's been shotgunned, but if you got any doubts on it, ask her."

Nobody said a word. And nobody moved to see inside Sally Gal's old place. They all just stood staring at me, some thoughtful, some scared maybe, but none of them friendly.

I figured I better start moving before they did. Raised my voice some and called out. "Fingers, I want to see you about a dog. And is that Brownie Davis with you?" I tried to sound like I meant it, but I felt a whole lot better about the situation when they melted away and made themselves distant.

"Anybody wants me, I'll be at the livery a spell." I untied Bucky from the rail, concentrating to keep my hands steady. "You got question or comment, find me there. I ain't hiding."

Casual as I could, I turned my back on the whole crowd and walked away, leading Bucky behind me to discourage any back-shooting.

It worked. Nobody tried to stop me nor dangle me from a tree. As I tuned into Gunder's barn, I took a fast look back, and the crowd was still there, discussing the whole thing, and already losing interest in me and the dead strangers.

I took a big, long breath, and it felt so good I took another. I was considering I could make a habit of it when old Heber Snow come running up as soon as he saw me.

"Streak Wilson! Young'n Streak! Dang, you're a sight for these tired old eyes. Danged if you ain't!"

He always was free with that word.

Old Heber used to help Bart Gunder around the livery, but I never had much use for him myself, on account of he was pretty much useless. But dang myself it was good to see him. I pumped his hand, called him an ornery old cuss, and looked around.

I said it before. Like everywhere else in Gunder's Station, the livery had seen better days. The walls were cracked and broken in a couple places where horses had kicked. The ladder up to the loft was missing some rungs, and the whole place just needed a good cleaning. Back in the back, someone was forking hay into stalls for animals that sounded like they needed it.

"Where's Bart hiding?"

"Oh, he ain't hiding," Heber never could tell when words were spoke in jest. "He's just gone."

About that time, the man forking hay left off and came up to join us. It was Harvey, with his sleeves rolled up and mud on his boots. I tried not to look surprised, but it's hard to hide anything from the Devil.

"Looked like the old guy here could use a little help," he said, "Got stuck with the place. Seems as how Bart wanted to visit his daughter—she lives a few days' ride from here; town called Retrospect. Anyway, he told Heber here to take care of things, said he'd be gone about a week. That was near a year ago, and nobody's seen nor heard from Bart Gunder since."

"I know I ain't done much of a job of it," Heber looked down at the ground around his feet. "Lot of work for one man, and I ain't handy…"

Something come across my mind. I walked over to where there was a kicked-out hole in the wall. "Let me see what I can do with this."

"I'll give you a hand with it." Harvey fetched around for tools.

CHAPTER 11

That's how it started. And looking back, it didn't last long, really. But that time I spent helping Heber Snow fix up Bart Gunder's livery was a few days of pure treasure. A time when I could forget about guns and killing, maybe just all-over stop thinking, and put my mind to measuring, cutting, hammering, and cleaning. And at night when I laid me to rest, I tried not to think about Sally Gal.

The Devil pitched right in beside us—well, beside me mostly, seeing as how the animals kind of shied away from him—and he turned out to be a good hand with a cross-cut saw and a short-handle sledge, which was a good thing too, because I said it before, old Heber was pretty much useless. He could cook, though. Not real good, but purely edible, and when it got too dark to work, he always had something readied-up hot to fill our bellies up.

Another good thing: that girl Kelly, the one from the saloon, she came by looking for work. Kind of on the small side for handling horses, but Harvey showed her how to work the forge, how to bend a bar on the anvil, fit a horseshoe or make a chain, and the girl learned quick.

We had us some notion for a while that Kelly had ought to do the meal-fixing around there, her being female and all, even if she was just a young'n. Turned out, though, her cooking was as close to poison as it could get and not kill a man outright. And when I say Poison, I don't mean the merciful poisons that put you to sleep and carry you off; I'm talking about the gut-busting, body-wracking kind of poison that makes a man repent of his sins one by one and cry out for death to end his suffering.

Kelly's cooking was like that.

So Heber cooked for all of us, and afterwards Kelly cleaned dishes while we men sat around the room, smoking and supervising her work.

Then we got to telling tall stories, partly to entertain ourselves, but mostly out of wickedness—we wanted to see how easy-fooled the girl might be. Come to find out later, maybe I got fooled myself by the stories that was told on those nights. Just tote it up to the things a body doesn't expect till they fall right down around his head.

Anyhow, that first night, Harvey told an old Comanche yarn, about how ghosts could get inside each other:

"The way this legend goes is that there's this dead Comanche, his name's Proud Eyes, because he sees so far and so sharp that sparks fly out of his eyes and light up whatever he's looking at." Harvey paused so Heber could get hold of it in his head. "So naturally, he was a great hunter, but he got to be so proud about it, always telling everyone what a great hunter he was, and how he never missed a shot in his life, that when he died, the braves in the next world didn't want to let him into Comanche heaven—whatever that is—and they told him he couldn't get into the big medicine lodge up yonder until and unless he killed a white buffalo."

That's all it took to get Kelly interested and Heber fascinated, and I was kind of liking the story too, so Harvey went on:

"Yeah, it seems this here Comanch', he was a great hunter all right, but he lost an arm whilst getting dead, so he could see game but not shoot it, and so he went moping around the Happy Hunting Ground, or wherever not-quite-heaven is in Comanche territory, till he met up with another dead Indian, and this one, he was named Proud Arms, because he was mighty strong—there's something about how he put the mountain passes where they are just by punching through 'em, 'cause he was too tired to walk around or climb over. But that part takes too long to tell.

"And Proud Arms, he was just as much in love with himself as Proud Eyes was in love with *himself*, and when he died, nobody up there in the spirit world wanted to let him in, so they gave him that White Buffalo business because, well, he's dead, see, and he's got him two good arms, only (You guessed it.) he messed up his eyes doing whatever he did to die of, and he can't see where to use those strong arms of his. So the rest of the dead braves figured they could rest easy and never worry about Proud Eyes nor Proud Arms either crashing their party.

"I reckon you can tell the story yourself here. What happens next, these two jaspers join themselves up, so one gets inside the other one's body till they're part one and part the other, and together they're mean as hell: big, strong, and not to be trifled with, and pretty soon the two-in-one kill them a white buffalo. And when they haul the carcass up to the pearly gates, Old Saint Powwow, or whoever does guard duty there, he tells them to come on in.

"But the way this story goes is that they weren't called Proud Eyes and Proud Arms for nothing. Both of 'em wanted to go first, and neither one of 'em would get out of the body they shared and let the other one go ahead, so they commenced to fighting, both of 'em still in the same body, with Proud Eyes flashing lights all over, and Proud Arms throwing punches that echoed off the mountains, and like I say, they're locked together, and maybe you figured out by now that's where Thunder and Lightning come from, and why one never can show up without the other.

"Or so the Comanches say."

CHAPTER 12

Next day, maybe it was the tale-telling loosened her up, but Kelly got to talking about herself.

It was a story like you hear a lot of out here. Her folks headed West from Tennessee after the War, her mother came down with a sickness—Kelly wasn't sure what, but it was fast and fatal, and right on the end of that, Kelly got herself bit by a rabid coyote.

"I was powerful sick for… I don't know, seemed like months where I couldn't eat, hardly moved, and you can see I still got scars where he cut up my hand…" She rolled back her sleeve and showed me her arm, and I'll tell the world and surrounding counties, it was not a pretty sight. Looked like somebody had took a broken bottle to it and just stirred it up like heavy paint, with little blobs in it.

I wasn't listening close to what she said next, more wondering if Sally Gal's face would be like that, and kind of a sickness went through me.

Kelly went on to say how she was still sick when her Pa got a chance to light out for the Black Hills gold strike, but he had to move fast, so he left Kelly with a distant cousin name of Stilson, which would be the Barkeep who put her to work.

"... Ain't heard from Pa since he left me here, but he never was one for writing, so I guess he's all right. And the work... well I didn't work there for long, but it was okay till those four men come in and pitched camp there. Ornery cusses."

That got my attention. "Pitched camp, you say?"

"They sure did. There always at least two of them hanging around the place—till you came in and killed 'em."

"I only killed just one of 'em. Try and remember it right."

"Sorry Mister Wilson."

"You say they all showed up at once?"

"That was kind of funny." She got to looking thoughtful over it. "I seen two of them come in on the north road, about an hour apart, and another come up from the creek east of here. Don't know about the fourth, but they all come into the bar there, one at a time, like, and each one of them, he looked the place over careful and close. First they acted like they didn't know each other, but I could see pretty soon it was just acting. And they asked Mister Stilson if he'd seen a man recent with a scar in his hair—I mean like that white streak you got. Then they asked me, too."

"What'd you tell them?"

"I... I told them how there's talk about you here, but I never seen you."

"What'd they do then?"

"Nothing. Just hanged around like they was waiting."

"I reckon they were."

"And I guess I figured that out, too. They was laying for you, wasn't they?"

"Seems like it."

"And you faced up to all four of 'em!"

"Yeah, but if I'd had a choice, or even knew what was in there, I wouldn't of walked into a thing like that. Nor even come near to it."

Only I didn't have a choice, and I never did. Because these men had been waiting for me to show up here. Just waiting, like buzzards wait for dead meat to ripen. And they were strangers to me.

Something about it gave me a nasty tingle at the back of my neck. The kind you get when there's something bad coming up behind you that you don't see till it's too late.

CHAPTER 13

That night it was old Heber's turn to give out with a story, and he starts in with, "This ain't no actual ghost story, it's just something I heard once. I couldn't even say I heard it for true, but I think I did, and this is the best I can remember to tell it.

"What I heard was about dead folks. And the fella was telling me this, he says there's some so bad, when they die, they just naturally can't get to Heaven, 'cause of they sinned so terrible, but they can't make their way to Hell, neither, 'count of those sins of theirs is just too heavy to carry.

"So there they is, not living and not dead. Hungry and they can't eat, thirsty and can't drink. They ain't mortal men nor ghosts neither. Walking the Earth, trying to get all the way to one place or the other, wandering..."

"I've heard how Injuns say something like unto that," Kelly near-whispered, "Like Mister Harvey was saying last night. How sometimes if some folks dies, they gotta wander between the winds, trying to find peace."

"The ancients had notions like that, too," Harvey said, "In the old stories, maybe their gods had just got up in a bad mood that day, or somebody'd do something just pure awful, and whoever it was would spend his eternity in the next world just wandering in the dark."

Heber got back to his story—if it was a story. "What was said to me, these restless spirits, they walk around sometimes like you and me, solid flesh and blood. Other times, they'll be like ghosts; they turn invisible and walk through walls, and all like that there. And all the time dead, but not departed-like. And here's the part that scared me good," He got a serious look on his face. "These things, they know if they ever got completely dead, they'd go right to Hell. So they's trying, all the time trying, to stay on in this world."

"How do they do that?" Kelly's eyes had got wide as silver dollars, and she talked in a whisper.

"They hire on at a livery," I said, "Then one day the owner tells them to look after the place whilst he's gone..."

"And he just ups and never comes back," Harvey laughed, "So old Heber got stuck here!"

We all of us had a good laugh then—all but Kelly, 'cause she thought we were laughing at her, which maybe we was, but she tried to look like she'd never been took in by it.

"Awwww, you men's full of beans! There ain't no such of a thing."

"I wouldn't know on it." Heber shook his head. "I'm just telling what I got told."

"Then what's their names?" Kelly challenged. "What do they call 'em?"

"It's hard saying," Harvey scratched his chin, and he was dead serious now. "Closest thing is the Indian words for 'em; it's hard to pronounce and doesn't quite fit right anyhow."

"What's the words?"

"You fixing to marry one or something?" Harvey could see mutiny and rebellion on that girl's face, so he raised a soothing hand, bummed tobacco and papers off me and got him a smoke going—he always makes a show out of that—before he went on: "the Sioux words sound something like Noodlesoup, and they almost translate as *One Who Walks In His Tree.*"

"Whaaah?"

"See these red men, some of 'em believe in laying their departed to rest in trees. So I guess it'd be more in the spirit to say *One Who Walks In His Grave.*"

"That takes too long to say. Just call them GraveWalkers."

I swear, Harvey's eyes twinkled when he looked down at Kelley. "GraveWalkers, it is, Missy." He blew a smoke ring. "GraveWalkers."

CHAPTER 14

"You have disappointed me, Mister Klavinsky."

Pug Klavinsky glanced from wobble-headed Hinchley to the squat, near-inert, Slasher Jim Trask, and felt his mouth go dry. "The boys done the best they could. Wilson was just too many for 'em. I told you—"

"You told me you'd send men who could do the job. And I paid you accordingly."

"I figured they could handle it." Pug could feel it again, something powerful and uncanny between Hinchley and Trask, linking them together...

"And I said at the time the price seemed steep." Hinchley's head rolled as he spoke. Klavinsky shivered openly, unable to hide it now.

"My boys—"

"Yes. Your boys. Two of them shot each other, two came back here to say they turned and ran."

"I guess so."

"Where are they now?"

"Down at the Snake Ranch, I reckon, Maybe up at Nola's Hurdy-Gurdy. They said Wilson looks like he's settling in there at Gunder's Station. You want to talk to 'em yourself?"

"At Nola's establishment?"

"I think maybe they're sharing a—"

"Mister Trask and I shall pay them a visit."

"Yessir."

"But not to talk."

"They say Wilson's working at the livery like he means to stay."

"I did not pay you to find gainful employment for Streak Wilson."

"Nossir."

"I paid you to have him killed. You took my money for it."

"Yessir."

"And he's still alive."

"He is."

"That means you owe us a life."

Klavinsky tried to answer and found his throat too dry to speak.

"Yours or his." Trask went on. "I want one or the other. I'd prefer Wilson's, but I told you before ..."

He used his hand to point his face to Slasher Jim Trask, and Pug felt it even stronger, that magnetic force between the two. Hinchley guided his face back, directly at Klavinsky.

"We're not choosy."

CHAPTER 15

Next afternoon late, Kelly and Harvey were patching up a kicked-out stall whilst I cleaned out the loft, and their voices carried up to me.

"Y'know, Mister Rideout, that Mister Wilson, it's hard to believe all the things what's said about him."

"Then don't." I could hear the smile in Harvey's voice.

"Don't what?"

"Don't believe them. Get to know the man and decide for yourself what's true about him."

"Talk has it he's powerful wicked. I heard the preacher once say a sermon against him. How he shot down an old crippled man in the street and brought ruination down on Gunder's Station."

"Well, you've seen him over the course of these last few days," the Devil said, "Does he strike you as the kind of man who'd do a thing low-down like that?"

"Folks say he makes deals with the Devil."

"Not lately. Oh, maybe once or twice, a long time back, but he hasn't done anything like that for years now."

"Really? He actual made a deal with the Devil?"

"Well, he was young then, and the fact is, he got snollygostered into it. The Devil never got his soul, though—not so far, anyhow—and that counts for a lot these days."

I came down from the loft.

"Harvey, what in tunket are you selling this trusting child?"

"She ain't as trusting as all that." The Devil brushed loose straw off his shirt. "Are ya, Kelly?"

"Guess I know a story when I hear one." She didn't sound real sure about it, though. I laughed and said I reckoned she might as well wash up for supper.

"Yessir!"

Harvey watched her head off to the pump by the trough. "She won't mind missing a little work!"

I looked at him. "That question I asked you, Harve'. Guess I meant it serious."

"How's that?"

"I asked what are you selling that girl? I'd hate to see her get took like I was."

"You injure my sensitive feelings, friend. Gimme some makings to compensate." I handed him tobacco and papers, which I keep handy when Harvey's around, on account of I guess there's none of that down in Hell.

"I'm capable of some low-down things." He rolled a cigarette one-handed and lit it with his finger. "That's more or less my job, you know. But every business has its ethics, and I'm not one to take advantage of a child. I'm a bit surprised you haven't seen it in me. Or figured it out, anyhow."

"Maybe I should have. Only I seen you talking to her about deals and got to wondering."

"Just good business. My reputation's bad enough without baby-snatching. Besides, she's got nothing I can use." He blew a smoke ring. "You weren't much older than her when we met— recall? But you were already respected for your shooting, and a partner like you would have put some shine on my own prestige." He raised an eyebrow to me. "And it still might, you know!"

Something about how he said that, it gave me a deep-down shiver. I mean to say we've rode together some, and I like his company, but there's times Harvey can be downright scary.

But it didn't last long. Heber called us in for supper and we found Kelly there ahead of us, washed up and setting plates out. Harvey got himself sat down whilst Heber filled his plate.

"Say, young lady." He turned to Kelly. "You given much thought to the future? Where you want to stay and earn your keep?"

"Figured I'd stay right here," She started moving food from her plate to her mouth. "I kind of cotton to this work."

"How'd you like to ride back with us and see about a job in Contention or thereabouts?" I asked.

She looked down at her plate. "I guess not."

I wasn't expecting she'd say that, and it set me back a step or so. "I could likely get you a job working for Wells Fargo. Office work."

"You best listen up, Kelly," Heber put in. "I like havin' you around, but there's more chances for a young woman elsewheres. Not much of a future here in Gunder's Station."

"Not much future here at all," Harvey echoed.

"There's a tomorrow here," Kelly kept staring down at her plate. "And the next day."

I saw then what she meant and how right she was. She raised her face and her voice to the whole table. "Guess I'm better to stay here. I thank you for thinking on it, Mister Rideout. You too, Mister Wilson. But the only future where you're going is for them as survive the trip."

Harvey stopped with a spoonful of Supper halfway to his mouth. "You getting skittish lately?"

"Could be I am, Sir. I don't mind if you think I'm chicken-livered, and I got nothing against you fellas. Mister Wilson, you got the way about you, you have. But I see it safer to put distance between us." She choked up a little, remembering. "I seen Mister Stilson get hisself shot just for standing too close to you."

"Young lady, you have a point there." Harvey looked from her to me. "Streak, it's risky business just sharing your shadow lately."

Yeah, it was. And it hit me kind of hard all over, how I wasn't safe to be with now. I looked around the table at Harvey, Kelly, old Heber… And the only one safe in my company was the Devil himself.

"You're talking good sense, Kelly," I said. "Time me and Harvey headed out to where we're going, anyhow."

"Back to Contention?"

"Nope, heading off to East Fork Swing Station. Something I promised myself to get done."

She got a look on her face that didn't belong on a little girl. "Is there killing mixed up in it?"

"I'm afraid there is."

"Then you best put some miles between us before somebody comes along to finish it for you."

"That's good thinking, Missie," The Devil said, "You'll go far."

"I'll stay right here."

An hour later, Harvey and me was packed up and ready to make tracks. Kelly and Heber had got our horses saddled, and they was standing by when we mounted up.

I looked down at Kelly a long while. Not fourteen years old yet, and wise as old King Solomon's great grandma. Or smart enough to steer clear of me, anyhow.

"You never told us a story," she said, "Uncle Heber and Mister Rideout did, but we never heard one from you."

"Don't actually have time for storytelling right now..." I started.

"Then tell a short one!"

I gave it some thought. Nothing came to mind off-hand. Then—

"I'll tell you about where we're headed," I pitched my voice to sound important and mysterious. "And *why*!"

"Is it scary?"

"Might be," I said, "That's the puzzlement of it; nobody knows!"

"You're funning me."

"I'm serious as Sunday," I pointed at the Devil. "Harvey here'll back me up, 'cause I'm headed out to guard a valuable load… only nobody knows what's in it—not even the jasper that sent it!"

"You *are* funning me!"

I turned to Harvey. "Am I funning the lady?"

"Well, strictly speaking, Miss, the gentleman who arranged to ship his item with Wells Fargo did know what it was. But rest his soul, he's dead now."

"What's he dead from?"

"That's the mystery part." I said, "Two days after he shipped out this parcel, he committed suicide."

"He destroyed himself." It was funny how Harvey said that like he was correcting me, but I didn't put any meaning to it till a lot later, and then it become something I'd sleep better not knowing.

But right then, I was meaning to make tracks.

"Goodbye, Kelly."

"Goodbye, Mister Wilson." Something in how she said that, the look on her face, seemed like she wanted to say a lot more.

But all she added on was, "I won't forget you."

CHAPTER 16

Sometime past two o'clock in the morning, things were quiet at Nola's Hurdy-Gurdy.

But there were two new quiet things, silent presences moving about the ornate furnishings and plush bedrooms of the House that never was a Home.

Hinchley and Trask came in the side door like a malevolent fog, oozing noiselessly through the doorway, across the hall, and up the stairs. They paused for a moment on the second-floor landing and sniffed the air like a wolf on the scent of a frightened animal.

The men they were after were asleep in the nearest room to the right, spread out naked on a big, overstuffed bed, with a woman between them. There were no locks on the doors. Nola had found that simpler all around. But someone—either Fingers Flanagan or Brownie Davis—had left a bottle and glasses on a tray just inside the door.

Not by accident. Fingers and Brownie shared the sleeping patterns of hunted men.

Hinchley and Trask came in silently anyway.

Across the room, in bed on the side closest to the door, Brownie Davis stirred, snorted, put a hand on the fleshy thigh of the woman he and Flanagan had earlier shared between them.

Sweezie's a class act, he thought sleepily to himself. *"A five-dollar-a-night gal and worth every penny of it!*

He felt something like a cold wind inside the room and came awake immediately.

It wasn't soon enough.

There was something in the room. Something as tall as the man Hinchley. Hairy and muscular like Trask. But less than human.

It came across the room in one swift, silent step,

Three seconds later, there was nothing left alive in the room. But there was something moving.

The thing smiled.

Time to leave a message!

*   *   *

In and around the town of Contention, it got said (and believed) that Justice Hopkins was actively patronizing Nola's Hurdy Gurdy House when Ed "Shorty" Gossett, writer/ editor, chief typesetter and custodial engineer of THE CONTENTION HERALD told him his presence was needed in an upstairs room. All anyone can say for sure was that the dead were discovered there in the small hours before dawn, and Justice Hopkins was at the scene just a few minutes later.

"How many times do I have to tell you folks that I'm not here to handle trouble? I'm here to adjudicate the law, and you aren't paying me for..." Hopkins stared at the sight he'd been summoned to see, and felt very small.

"Come down off the ramparts, General," Gossett yawned. "Miss Nola just thought you ought to warm your eyes on this before we decide what to do about it."

"When you tell me it's dead men with their necks...I got to just naturally assume—" He looked away as best he could, but his eyes were drawn helplessly back.

"—Murder," Gossett supplied.

"And while I'm perfectly capable of trying a man for capital crime—" Hopkins tried to gather stream again."—the apprehension and detention of such miscreant must—"

"Must be on somebody else's plate of beans. I know that. Miss Nola knows it. Hell, the whole town could likely repeat it from memory, as many times as you've said it."

Hopkins crossed the room quickly to open a window and get some air, but it was latched and locked.

"Won't open Judge," Gossett said. "I tried it."

"Yes!" Hopkins remembered that Miss Nola took pains to make sure nobody got in without paying admission. "I-uh-I heard about that. I mean, gentlemen in their cups have mentioned..."

"Quite right, your honor." Gosset stepped around a chair lying on the floor, picked up a broken piece of it, and showed it to the judge.

"First thing I had to do was get in here. Wasn't easy. Somebody'd pushed this chair here under the doorknob."

Hopkins studied the broken chair. "We'll admit that into evidence." He looked around. No signs of struggle in the room. Just three people lying neatly together on the room's generous bed, fully dressed, arms folded solemnly across their breasts, heads tilted at an unnatural angle, and on each face, a look of

"How would you describe it?"

"You're the writer," Justice Hopkins tried to look away from the bodies and couldn't. "What would you call the looks on those faces?"

"I couldn't say for sure. I mean, hard to tell with their necks… Like I told you."

"That's certain."

"They look scared—"

"Damn scared."

"But there's more…" The editor was already trying to frame the words for tomorrow's paper. "Something more… Ever come across anything like this in those fancy books you read?"

"I wouldn't read any book with this in it. Nor anything like it. I just don't know how to say it…" Justice Hopkins was a careful man with words. But now he found them spilling out, and he himself helpless to stop the flow.

"But wait. Maybe…" A memory came back to him. "Back during the War, a bunch of us in the Home Guard, we were chasing down a Mexican—"

"You were in the Home Guard?"

"Yes, but if you print anything on that subject, I'll kill you and sue your rightful heirs for malicious libel. I've left that life behind me, thank you.

"At any rate, this Mexican had killed a lady—nasty, it was—and so we got after him, and he hied himself into the Badlands there south of Lubbock, and I tell you, Gossett, that man spent a week just dodging around in the rocks, laughing at us, while we hunted and chased and never got close to catching him. Hell's hinges man, we never even got close to the smell off his saddle. And him jumping here, there, and all over, and us—"

"Hopkins," Gossett broke in. "This is a good story, but I'd admire to know if it ends up anywhere close by the neighborhood of this here present situation."

"I'm just getting to it now. Well, after about a week of this, half the posse decided they had pursued this felon long enough, and time to go home. The other half decided to chase him for a while longer yet, so the two groups split up. And Gossett, I'm damned if we didn't catch him between us! He came out onto the open plain just as those of us that were leaving got in front of him, and those still chasing him pulled up behind.

"As I say, he'd just come out in the open, and the look on his face—I'll never forget it. Surprised, of course. And scared of what was going to happen next, because lynching never is an easy death, and his surely wasn't." Hopkins paused, looking for the right words, then went on: "But there was something else too. I saw it on his face. It was *realizing!*"

Hopkins looked down at the three dead faces, then back up to Gossett.

"Don't you see it? This murderous, thieving miscreant realized he'd picked the wrong trail to ride, and he saw it for the first time that he'd chosen the wrong way to go, and now there was no turning back." He gestured toward the three bodies. "Gone wrong and no way back."

Gossett stared quietly for a long moment. Then another, longer. He shivered and tried to shake the chill off his soul.

"You never told me that story before."

"I never got the point of it until just now."

"And you really don't want me to print any of it."

"Mister Gossett, if dead Mexicans could talk, this one would be screaming it from his grave."

"Well then, just answer me one thing, if you would."

"If I can."

"You heard me say I had to get that chair out from under the doorknob to get in here."

"I did."

"And you yourself tried to open that window—the only other way to get in or out of this room—and found it locked. Did you not?"

"Mister Gossett," Hopkins raised his chin and assumed a dignity unusual for a man in a whorehouse. "I can see where you're leading with this line of questioning, and I shall order it stricken from the record."

CHAPTER 17

"Looks like a good night for riding."

Moonrise had just got around to Gunder's Station, and it lit up the fresh-painted walls on the livery barn like something else I read in a book; the fella who wrote this said about how the palaces was *'Bathed in moonlight'* and if there's better ways of saying that, I can't think what they'd be. The Devil looked around us and smiled. "All fed and rested—us and the mounts both—and a moon so bright you could read the newspaper by it!"

"It's all that." I felt a gentle breeze at my back and got me a notion. "Reckon I'll swing by the graveyard on the way out and get a look at my marker."

A few years back, I bought a tombstone for a man name of Pablo Schopenhauer, on account of he saved my life once, and also on account of he was dead and needed one. Anyhow, whilst I was at it, I bought me a marker against the day I'd want one for my own.

"You sure?" Harvey looked doubtful. No, he looked downright discouraging. "It's a little out of our way."

"Not much. I'm thinking we might swing down by Scogginsville on the way to East Fork. Maybe pick up some shells there, and such-like we can't get in Gunder's Station."

Harvey's face changed from doubtful to knowing. "Seems I recall you shoeing a mare for a peddler that passed through there recently."

"I disremember."

"Yes… Come to think on it, he said something about a new saloon opened up there."

"Did he?"

"Run by a woman, this fella said."

"That so?"

"Yes, but when somebody asked who ran it, he didn't know. Turned out he never even went in the place."

"Is that a fact?"

"Well, I guess there's worse pursuits than going from town to town just to see who's tending bar there."

"Won't hurt to look."

"But I still don't see any need to pass by the graveyard."

"It'll give us a chance to work the burrs out of these animals. Let's go!"

I put the spurs to Bucky, and he charged off like a youngster, running just for the pleasure of running, and sharing the joy of it. I couldn't help smiling myself.

Till I got to the cemetery and seen what they done to my grave.

There was *Here lies,* and then my name on it, *STREAK WILSON,* and below that was the writing I had the man carve into it:

Best shot in Ware County
Pray for his soul

Only someone had chiseled and burned and marked it up so's it read

Best kiler in Ware County
Ougt of hanged him
Burn in Hel!

And then somebody'd mule-kicked it, knocked it down, and broke it in half.

Harvey caught up to me whilst I was still looking down at the pieces. I let out a long, tired sigh. "You never once said *I told you so* to me, have you, Harvey?"

"No, sir, I have denied myself that small pleasure." He looked down at the broken headstone scattered on the ground. "Though I have to say, friend, there's been times when you put temptation square in my path."

I thought. *Me, tempting the Devil. Well there's a switch.*

But all I said was "Ozymandias."

"How's that?"

"Ozymandias. It's the name of a poem."

"Ah, yes. Something about a monument, wasn't it?"

"Yeah, that's it. I never much liked it, 'cause it don't rhyme good, but I can see his point now."

It's about this statue, see. There's this statue of a king, but all that's left is the feet. The rest of it's all got smashed up and blown away. And so's everything else, all around, smashed up and gone. There's nothing much left anywhere, for miles around. But at the bottom of what's left of that statue, it says something like, 'Hey everybody. *This is me. Now just look around and see all the great stuff I done.*' Only there's nothing of it left.

I thought on it some. "Can't remember who wrote it."

"I seem to recall Percy Shelley wrote that one."

"Kind of a soft-sounding name. No wonder I don't like his writing."

"He did tend to run on the gentle side, yes. But he ran with the wild ones, too." Harvey thought on it some. "From time to time, anyway."

"Makes a man think, anyhow."

"Yes. Well, let's not make a habit of it." He flicked his reins to head off, and Bucky fell in behind. "Not while we got hold of good riding weather."

Yeah, we rode on out, 'cause there was nothing else to do. I got to thinking on that dead king with his monument to Nothing in the middle of Nowhere, and me with a smashed headstone to remember me by. And that got me to wondering about that little girl, Kelly. How she said she'd never forget me.

Something in her voice when she said it, final-like.

That's when I got the idea. Figured it all out and saw it plain., She was staying there in that dead-end town, I was going to East Fork.

But it was me that was getting nowhere.

We covered some ground that night—well, I guess it was morning really, being past Midnight, but we hadn't gone far when maybe Harvey noticed I was kind of quiet, and he asked. "You worked out any answers about that welcome committee that met you at the saloon?"

"Kelly said they were new here, and they showed up looking to find me. So that means somebody sent them."

"Who do you figure for that?"

"Not clear sure for certain on it yet. Pug Klavinsky wants me dead, only he's too gutless to do the work himself. He might of sent 'em, only..." I pondered a while. That's another word I learned: *ponder*. It means to wonder about something a lot. That's why *ponder* and *wonder* sound alike.

"Only what?" Harvey snapped me out of it.

"Only last I seen of Pug, he was purely poverty-struck. Don't seem likely he could afford to hire any guns for a job— much less four of 'em."

"That would be why he took to tricking Christy Gorsuch into that bone-head play back in Contention."

"Likely enough." I pondered at it some more. "So the money to hire on extra hands came from..."

"Go on."

"Big Bob Banneker said there's a high-value load going out. Could be somebody besides Pug Klavinsky wants it. Somebody with cash money to hire on them dry-gulchers."

"He'd have to want it pretty bad." Harvey scratched his head over it.

"Stands to reason." I nodded. "Makes me kind of wish I'd asked what-all's in that special crate, anyhow."

CHAPTER 18

"**Y**ou've never heard of the Grand Grimoire." It wasn't a question, but Pug Klavinsky shifted uneasily, as if Hinchley and Slasher Jim Trask expected an answer he couldn't think of.

"Nossir," he finally said.

"It's sort of a book. Sometimes called RED DRAGON, but only in spurious French editions. The true original is in Aramaic. Which means nothing to you."

Klavinsky could feel the scorn in Hinchley's voice, and it twisted inside him like a large and rather dull knife. But his only visible reaction was to fold his hands together—to stop them from shaking.

"What you need to know is what the Grimoire looks like. So listen attentively and remember well." As Hinchley spoke, Klavinsky tried to ignore the waves of energy—stronger than ever now—passing between Hinchley and the hairy abomination on the bed. He focused on his host's words: "... try to imagine a very old, very large, book. A book more than four hundred years old. Almost a yard tall, and more than half as wide. Perhaps eight inches thick. It will have wooden covers, silver hinges, and very very old, pages, yellowed and brittle with age. Can you imagine how it looks?"

"Yeah. I guess."

"Excellent! But you will not see any of this because the Grimoire will be wrapped in heavy cloth and packed up securely in a stout wooden crate. Do you understand?"

"I -uh- I reckon I do, yessir."

"Then listen even more closely now. I described the book to you only because I want you to know the approximate dimensions of the crate which will contain it. Is that clear?"

It wasn't at all, but Klavinsky nodded anyway.

"The crate will bear a destination label for a city in— Klavinsky, can you read?"

There was a long pause, then a grunt. "Some."

"Then let's just say that you will be looking for a crate approximately a yard tall, a yard wide, and a foot thick. The size and shape should be sufficient to identify the contents. You can picture it in your mind, can't you, Klavinsky?"

Pug couldn't. Couldn't create the image in his mind. But he could picture the consequences of a negative answer. "I surely can, Sir."

"But you shall under no circumstances open the crate. Is that very clear?"

"Sure."

"Very very clear?" Hinchley's eyes spoke of slow, painful death. And they seemed positively kindly in the same room with the look on Slasher Jim Trask's face.

Pug felt the shiver move from his spine to his hands once more and tried to hide naked fear.

"Yessir."

CHAPTER 19

"**W**hat's this-all, anyhow?"

Seemed like a good question at the time. Me and the Devil had been riding in easy stages since leaving Scogginsville, so as to get to the swing station at East Fork just ahead of sunrise without tiring the horses. When we caught sight of it, the station man was already harnessing up a team—but not to a stagecoach. He was hitching up to a wagon loaded with square wood crates -- and Big Bob Banneker was tightening straps across the wagon bed to lash down the load.

I lit down off Bucky and gave 'em a hand just by way of polite courtesy, and I asked 'em just by way of being purely bewildered.

"What's this-all, anyhow?"

"Heathen bones." Big Bob tied off the last stretch of leather, while the station man—a sight older than me, but not as tall—wiped dust off himself. "Obliged for the help." He put out a dusty hand for me to shake. "The name's Jensen. Squat Jensen. You'd be Wilson, wouldn't you?"

"Streak Wilson." I shook a tough, leathery hand and nodded over at the Devil. "This here's Mister Harvey Rideout."

I turned to Big Bob at the wagon bed. "And I guess I don't know what you mean by Heathen Bones." I took me a longer look at them crates.

I'd say each one was about three feet long, and maybe two foot high by two foot wide, and there must have been a couple dozen stacked in that wagon.

"Just what I say." Big Bob cleared his throat and spit dust on the ground. "These crates are each one of 'em packed with the bones from a heathen Chinese." He paused. "But not all of them."

We walked into the swing station, and Bob went on: "Your particular crate with the valuable load is down in the middle of it all, and if you dig down far enough you can spot it easy on account of it's some smaller than the others. I figured to pack it on the bottom, underneath all the rest, to hide it good."

"You're a sharp one, Big Bob." Harvey looked over the wagon and gave it a lop-sided grin. "I know you never cared much for my company, but you've got brains and no denying it."

Big Bob just grunted. Jensen took a sharp look at Harvey, but didn't seem like he saw anything objectionable. "Let's get us some coffee till the driver shows up."

That East Fork station wasn't much, but not many of them are. Just one big room with a table, stove, and a couple of narrow army cots. There was a couple blankets hung on a rope separating the cots from the rest of the place to give it the look of being two rooms, but I don't think it ever fooled anybody.

Big Bob checked his watch as we headed inside. "Driver shoulda been here by now. Blondie Ribbins don't run late as a rule, and he was s'posed to have left Contention four hours back."

Squat waved us towards a bench to sit on and poured out some reasonable-tasting coffee. Harvey took a sip. "I think maybe I heard about those Chinese bones you mentioned, Mister Banneker. Mighty interesting."

"Heathen deviltry, more like." Big Bob said it to the room in general, like he wasn't really talking to Harvey. "But I don't fuss my head over it. Someone pays good money to take these here dead Chinamen and ship 'em west, well, I just go and get it done. Or at least that's what I'll go and do if Blondie ever gets here."

"I think they like to be called Chinese, not Chinamen." Harvey grinned a little wider.

"I don't suppose they care what you call them now." Bob talked into his coffee.

I finished mine and thought about pouring me some more, then decided not to in case the driver showed up sudden. But I was starting to get a feeling about that.

"They going to Hell anyhow," Jenson put in helpfully, "Them dead Chinese."

"Going to Hell you say?" Big Bob walked to the window and studied the road, looking for sign of our stage-driver. "All of 'em?"

"Them's the rules." Squat walked over beside him and that made two of them looking for Blondie Ribbins, but it didn't help none.

I looked to see how Harvey felt on this kind of talk, and he smiled like the way a man does when he's listening to a funny story, only he's heard it before.

"Only way to get to Heaven is to get with Jesus." Squat said. "Says it in the Bible, and that's final."

"What do you say, Mister Rideout?" Bob turned away from the window. "All those dead yellow men out there packed up in boxes; are they heaven-bound?"

Harvey gave him that look right back and raised him a Dollar. "I wouldn't know, Mister Banneker. Heaven's none of my concern."

Time to cool things down, I figgered. "Bob, what's in the crate you hid under the others?"

He must of seen what I was trying at, and I guess he thought it was a good idea. "I'm not certain-sure of it, but I think it's some kind of a book."

"You saying Somebody's paying you special rates to ship a-a *book*?"

"Seems like it to me."

Now I like books myself, but it'd never cross my mind to spend a lot of money over one. "What gives you that notion?"

"Just that a rich collector down along the Mexico line packed that little crate, sealed it tight up, paid Wells Fargo a handsome figure of money to escort same to a little town a half day's ride from here called Retrospect, where some experts are—What was it the feller said? Oh yeah—*'to examine the contents under approved conditions and verify or disprove their authenticity.'* Then if it passes muster, they'll send it on to New York, and from there to wherever the Pope lives."

"The Pope?" Squat stopped looking out the window and stared at Big Bob. "He wants to read it?"

"Naaah, he's just going to keep it in some kind of museum. So I reckon it's a scarce book. You ever hear the like of that, Streak?"

"Guess I never did." I turned back to the window. Knew sure as sunrise in the mountains there was nobody coming— not just yet, anyhow-- but I couldn't help trying another look-see. "Can't see much sense anyhow in buying a book and no gumption to read it."

Squat shook his head. "Book museums... Chinese bones... The world's just getting too complicated for a man these days. Never heard of moving dead bodies around like this-here."

"It's a special thing with the Chinese." Harvey got a thinking-look on his face. "Seems important to them to get buried with their ancestors. They call it repatriation of bones."

"Fancy words." Squat looked out the window again, and I guessed he was getting the same antsy feeling about that driver like I had.

"Means a lot to 'em, no matter what you call it." Harvey started, but all of a sudden no one was listening. Not even Harvey. We were all of us looking out the window now, at company coming into the yard.

That "company" was more like a sight they charge you a dime to look at under a tent. First in line was an old Mexican leading a burro. Dusty, sweaty, tired, and patient-looking—man and beast both.

Then come a lady perched on the burro, likewise Mexican, and I'll say she was a fine-looking woman, dressed like she'd spent a lot on clothes and sure got her money's worth. Pretty, too; perfect-pretty, like the lady on a soap wrapper, with soft dark hair and skin like polished marble.

But all those fine looks was wasted, 'cause she had this proud look all over, sitting like that burro was a throne and the rest of the world could be her kingdom till something nicer come along. She was dusty, too—nobody rides that country without collecting a whole lot of it on him—but most of her dust was riding on a wide-brimmed sombrero and long, new-looking leather duster that stretched clear down to a shiny pair of fancy boots.

The parade rolled on, and there was another man riding behind that royal-looking lady, another Mexican, almost as well-dressed as she was. And even he never got more than what the books call a passing glance from any of us.

Because he was holding a six-foot pole, and there was a head on the end of it, tied on by its own long yellow hair.

Big Bob must of known right off it was his driver, on account of he drew in his breath and gave out with a hoarse whisper, "Blondie Ribbins!"

Squat Jensen added, "And he's got Pepe Avocado and the Queen of Salomey with him!"

CHAPTER 20

"I espied this unfortunate pate lying recumbent in the road." The fancy Mexican who Squat Jensen called Pepe Avocado—I never did learn if that was his right name or not— leaned on a corral rail while the old one tended his animal and the rest of us tried not to stare at the fresh-chopped head, still on the end of a pole, propped up against a fence post. "Perhaps two miles distant, as one leaves behind Rock Hill Valley. And I conjectured *how came he to take his rest here?* Of course, he said nothing. Silence is the way of such as he. The lady whom I have the honor to escort, *Señorita* Maria Sophia Vales affected to see nothing, yet I could sense her displeasure. There was movement of some sort in the rocks above—man or animal I could not determine—so we did not tarry, lest we share his fate. I had old Juano affix to his golden locks *el palo largo*— Forgive me, I mean to say *the long pole of wood*." He waved at the head like he was pointing at a guy in a saloon. "And we convey-ed him thus. He is, you say, the wagon driver?"

"He was," Squat stared up at the dangling head. "Up till just recent." He scratched his own head for reassurance. "What's your thinkin' on this, Bob?"

Banneker put his eyebrows together. "I'm trying to figure out somebody else's thinking, and calculate as to who abridged him like that."

"*Abridged?*"

"It means cut short," I said.

"Well, that fits the situation."

"And it means there's somebody —" Big Bob peered down the road toward Rock Hill Valley. "—Somebody meaner than snakes, and probably more'n one of 'em—layin' up in the rocks, just a-waiting for us to try and get this wagon past 'em."

I meant to say before how that fine-looking lady—that Maria Sophia Vales—she went straight into the swing station house soon's they got there, and she stayed inside. Come to find out later, she fixed herself a pot of tea and just sat there drinking it, cool as you please, whilst us men stood around the corral and discussed what to do about the situation, in between smokin', chewin', and cussin'.

At a time like this, folks just naturally look to Big Bob Banneker for orders and ideas. Other times, just for orders. But now it was him coming to me: "That how you figure it, Streak?"

"I'm figuring a lot of things," I looked over at Blondie Ribbins' fair-haired head, and it looked back at me. "Whoever left this in the road did it to stop us. The idea was that when Blondie didn't show, we'd eventual mosey out our own selves, likely with you driving." I nodded his way. "Right so far, Bob?"

"Right so far."

"And whereas… Well, think on it like this: if we saw a dead body in the road, we might could think it's somebody playing possum, meaning to stop us, and we'd think that and just keep on a-going. You follow me?"

"Yeah, but I don't like where you're headed," Banneker must've got tired of seeing that thing on the pole, 'cause he turned all of a sudden to Squat. "Hey, get a shovel, won't you?" Then back to me. "You're thinking whereas if we might not stop for a body laying in the road, was we to see this here head, just rolling around out there on company time, we'd likely stop to have a word with him and maybe offer a ride."

"As did I!" The elegant Mexican spoke up. "I completed just such of a performance."

"There's living proof," Banneker took a longer look at Avocado. "I think so, anyhow." Then back to me." So now what are we gonna do about the situation?"

"I got an idea," I checked my watch. Not even Seven yet. Plenty of time for this. "But you ain't gonna like it much. Nossir, you won't care much for it nohow."

CHAPTER 21

I got to say it warn't easy to take those two fancy Mexicans seriously. Not with that one called Pepe Avocado fussing over the beautiful lady, looking about like he worshipped her, and her treating him like the hired help. And it didn't help any that the two of them were dressed like this was some swanky cotillion.

So when we went back inside, and Pepe explained my plan to his lady, in between pouring her tea and seeing she was as comfortable as anyone could get in a swing station, she just never blinked an eye when he said, "I, of course, shall intend to accompany *Señor* Wilson."

I couldn't come back with any better answer than "Hunh?"

"Do I use the proper vocabulary? I have become instructed personally in the finest points, which I have acquired in your vernacular by means of education from an institution of higher learning, with scholars of expertise."

"Oh my stars," Harvey smiled, "He learned his English from College Professors."

"I understand you okay—I reckon." I looked around in my head for the right way to say this next part. "I just didn't figure on you volunteering on a job like this, *Señor* Avocado."

"The necessity only recently arrived," he spoke so calm it was right next to cold. "Perpend: yourself, *Señor* Wilson; you aggregate up to one person. Yet how many others may be totaling up themselves among the rocks? This we know not. So it is blatant that you and I must add up to two persons."

Squat Jenson looked like he was trying to read a book, but the print was too small. "You want to go out there with Streak?"

"You have misapprehended my words," Pepe broke in, "I do not *want* myself to go out there with the *Señor* Streak; I *insist* upon it. I have determined to become his associate in this employment."

I glanced over to see how *Dona* Maria was taking this. Looked to me like the biggest worry she'd have over him dying would be where to put the place cards at his funeral. I think Big Bob seen it too; started to shake his head, then thought better of it. "Whatever you say."

It was two hours later when the three of us—meaning Harvey, Pepe Avocado, and me—neared the jaggy outcrop they call Rock Hill Valley, close enough to worry about getting ourselves seen or heard, and reined up our mounts. Pepe and me pulled our saddle guns.

It had took that long to get us there by way of heading the other direction clear out of sight, then circling around to come in unexpected-like from the far side. Now we were closer-up, I could see how that stretch in front of us was pure Badlands: hard to get across, easy to get lost in, and smart to stay clear of.

So, of course, I was heading right into it.

It repays a man to know the folks around him, how they come to be there, and where they think they're going. So along the ride there, I asked Pepe about himself. And it didn't take this one long to warm up on the subject.

"I am of the *aristos*, the nobility of Spain, and among them, my family is enumerated among the oldest generations in Madrid."

Well, maybe, but he had the cheekbones like you see on a Yaqui, and some of the skin color too. Harvey just ignored all that, though.

"Blood to be proud of, *Señor*." He flashed his teeth. "And worthy of the fine *Señorita* you escort."

"She is my betrothed." He said it like he was trying to convince himself. I thought me back on how he looked at her and the way she looked back at him, and tried to say something nice about it.

"Makes you a lucky man."

"It is so. And I must be worthy of the honor."

"How's that?"

"I have studied hunting and riding, acquired the art of the blade, and aptitude with firearms of each variety. I have even acquainted some skill in hand-to-hand combat unarmed. All to become a man worthy of *la Dona* Maria Sophia Vales. A man fit for the game."

"What game we talkin' about?" I wondered if I was keeping up with the conversation.

"The game that is Life."

Now, I got to say that remark set me to thinking. This little half-an-hombre talking about how tough he thought he was, the way he hopped to her tune, and she seeming like she barely noticed he was there.

"And I am also quite the scholar," he went on, "I permeate the libraries, universities, even the monasteries and offices of newspapers, to gain observation and awareness."

"And collect big words?"

"Ah, you have ascertained it!" He sat up straighter in the saddle and looked pure proud. "I abruptly became familiar that just as the longest of bloodlines is revered among the proudest of families, so the scholar, the professor, the man of education, all gaze with respect on those who utilize only the most polysyllabic of the arcane vocabulary."

"More on length than strength, eh?" Harvey put in.

"Seems to me you got that right, Pardner."

"You said what?" Pepe shot us a look like he thought maybe we were making fun off of him, and didn't know if it was fightin' words, so I set to quiet him up some.

"Nothing, *Señor* Avocado. Just that you'd fit right in with those kind of educated folks."

"I respond appreciatively to you." He touched the brim of his wide sombrero to show he felt honored or something, like you'd tip your hat in respect.

"Don't mention it." Harvey looked him up and down and sideways. "But you got to pardon me if I say you don't quite seem like a fighting kind of man, and that's a fact. Meaning no offense."

"A man who will not fight is a coward." He said it like a hard-learned lesson. Then his voice got softer, like he was remembering something sad. "Or perhaps merely a fool to run away from what must come."

"Maybe so." I said, "And I know what you mean about running away, but I'd sooner ride with a man who'll walk away when he can." He gave me a look like I'd dropped a few notches on his measuring stick, but I went on. "You're going to find it damned inconvenient to look after this gal if you get yourself killed first."

"You crack wise words to me, sir. But I have made provision for her to acquire wealth-" He broke off of a sudden. "In the event of my extinction, she is well maintained."

I kind of wondered about that, on account of how this Pepe Avocado didn't look like rich folks himself. But when he talked again, the tone of his voice said Keep Out.

"Better to seek out a fight than to run from one."

"And best not to get seeked yourself." I signaled to hunker down and stay close behind me, cradled my long gun, crawled to the top of the closest ridge and raised my head slow and careful. "Let's see if we're still unexpected..."

Off to one side, I could just make out the dust raised by Big Bob and Squat driving the Fargo wagon, coming up the trail from the swing station, still a good mile or so from Rocky Hill Valley, still out in the open where they couldn't get snuck up on. Should be just about now...

I heard it: the sound of a wheel coming off and rolling away to god-knows-whereabouts.

"Time to move up," I kept my voice low. Pepe nodded and looked around.

"The other one is not among us. Your friend."

"Harvey? He's got a way of slipping out at times like this." We lowered us into a shallow arroyo and started making our way to the boulders that make up Rocky Hill. If I'd figured right, whoever was up there in the rocks would be looking the other way, down the road at the wagon, watching Squat Jensen—who was wearing my shirt and hat, and with a streak of flour paste in his hair to look like mine—they'd be watching him and Big Bob Banneker working to chase down the spun-off wheel and get it back on the axle, which promised to be a good hour's work, unless they could stretch it out some longer.

"Your *companero* leaves you alone by yourself at such as this moment?"

"He doesn't mix up in anything without he gets paid for his work. Now watch what I do and wait for me to signal."

I lifted myself up a mite, rolled out of the arroyo, and crawled across a short patch of dry ground without raising dust. Soon as I reached the nearest boulder, I squirreled around to one side and gave a quick peek overtop.

No sign that anybody'd seen us. I waved Pepe to join me, and he was every inch as slick-moving as me. He moved up close alongside and whispered,

"He is mercenary? Your friend?"

"You could say that."

"And still you regard him as a friend?"

"Best I got." I took a careful second look at the rocks above us. "Now let's us see if we can find any horses staked out. From here on, try to keep about twenty feet between us."

"Such is wise counsel."

"And it's good advice, too." There was a twisty trail between the boulders, and I took it slow, listening for dying echoes from rock walls, sniffing at tired breezes for the scent of horses.

It came as a sound. A sharp nicker from somewhere close and a short scuffle of hoofs. The noise of horses tied close up and getting restless. I waved Pepe to come up, and spoke softly when he got beside me.

"I heard horse-noise from just the other side of the next bend." I pointed to a gap between the boulders. "I figure to set here a minute and see if anybody tries to quiet it down."

"You evince sagacity," Pepe whispered back. "These men awaiting us. They are not ordinary cut-your-throats. They decapitated the driver, this Blondie person. And you surmise that they perpetrated it merely to impede the expedition of your wagon?"

"That and to shake us up considerable."

"They are bloody men we seek in these rocks."

"Well let's go see if we out-thunk 'em any. Move extra-careful now."

I slow-walked to the edge of the bend, made sure I wasn't throwing my shadow ahead of me, and eased around the corner.

Six horses, rope-corralled and getting antsy. I made myself breathe easy. A horse can sense tension in a man, same as a dog can, and it scares him. So I spoke soft and pointed my long gun down-ways.

"Easy now, you dumb brutes." I said it like I was humming a lullaby. "I'm gonna call my friend Pepe Avocado to come over here, real easy-going, and say howdy. Pepe? You want to come and be gentle with these crow-baits?"

He knew horses, Pepe did. Came in easy and smiling, soft-singing something like a Mexican love tune.

"There are no fewer than six, *mi compadre*," he crooned, "These are not favorable odds to gamble."

"Then we'll just deal from both ends of the deck," I crooned back at him. "Let's get past the animals. Gently now."

"We do not instigate the horses to flee, and thereby cut off the foe's retreat?"

"Not on your grand-daddy's shotgun we don't."

"And your motivation for this is … ?"

Truth to tell, my thinking was that these jaspers got us outnumbered, and if some of 'em felt like leaving the party early, I surely didn't want to slow 'em down any. But what I said to Pepe was, "No telling what those horses'll do if we get close enough to cut 'em loose, and I don't want to take the chance they might kick up a fuss and get us noticed. So let's try and get around 'em without that. Okay by you?"

"Sagacious."

"Gesundheit."

Seems Pepe had a way with horses, too. He slipped past them without making any stir and moseyed out like a stroll in the park. I guess that's when I begun to think this funny little cuss was a good man to have siding me.

And looking back, I'm sorry I didn't have him around later on.

CHAPTER 22

Right then I gave him a quick education in Ambush. "A man as wants to dry-gulch somebody just naturally hides himself for the job. So in this particular place, they'd get behind those rocks about twenty, thirty feet up." I pointed up to where I was talking about. "Looks like there's a natural ledge there, with plenty of boulders for cover, and our friends have likely stowed themselves somewhere like this, only on the other side of the hill, where the trail passes right under. You savvy?"

"Sometimes, yes. A man must do somewhat for it or go mad, you understand."

I would have paid a quarter just to find out what he thought "savvy" meant, and I wished I had time to ask him. I just motioned him to move as quiet as he could, and we started climbing.

Took us all of twenty minutes, or maybe even a half hour, but we did it without raising any attention, and when we got to a good place, we hunkered close and I pointed up higher, at the bald crest of the hill.

"Up there a man's in a better position, but there's nothing to get behind, and he's easy-seen from the road."

"And in that manner," Pepe picked up on it. "Itinerants from the station would in probability detect him in advance and become forewarned."

"So, if they're as smart as I figure on—and no smarter—we oughta be all by ourselfs once we get up to the top there, and in pretty good shape to look down and knock the competition off their perch."

"It is tactically sound."

"And an easy climb, too, so long as no one sees us doing it without we see them first."

"We commence at present?"

"Now."

It was harder climbing than I figured on, but five minutes later we'd got ourselves up to the top, and five minutes after that, we were lying prone on an overhang, looking down at a half-dozen specimens of gallows-bait hiding behind the rocks below, rifles ready, getting themselfs set for the kill. Six horses, six men. Good to see it all nice and tidy like that.

Big Bob and Squat Jensen had put on a good show; spent some time getting that wheel back on, but not long enough to get this bunch restless in their seats, nor suspicious about it. And now that they were on the move and drawing close, they were the main attraction in these parts.

I double-checked to make sure there weren't any strays, and spotted Pug Klavinsky in the audience. That wrapped it up neat and tight.

"I don't like it much," I said.

"You suspect a ruse?" Pepe had taken off his hat so the wide brim wouldn't show when we peeked from the overhang. Smart move, that. Now he put it back on to keep the sun off.

"No," I considered, "We covered ourselves good, and it was hard enough work getting here that nobody made it easy for us." I looked down at the bunch below. Even this far off there wasn't any of them looked worth a damn. They'd killed a man and cut his head off just for show, and every one of them looked hungry to do it again. "I just never much cared for back-shooting a man."

"Truly?" Pepe looked at me with eyes that said he understood. Then he sighted down the barrel of his long gun at the men below. "I myself have never sustained such a compunction."

He fired.

Below us, a man jerked, then slumped down against the rocks.

After that. I didn't have to worry about back-shooting nobody. They was all firing upwards at nothing and scrambling every which-way to nowhere.

And they mostly didn't get there.

One of them made for a gap betwixt the rocks. I got off a shot just as he dived into it, and got him on the hip as he slid down the crevice. A fat man right behind him started to follow, saw he wasn't going to make it, spun around, and took the time to spot us up there on the ledge and get me in the sights of his saddle gun. It was too much time. I chest-shot him and watched him flip sideways, fall across the gap, and fill it with his dead body. While I was at it, Pepe shot two more purely fatal. And right after that, the one I wounded made it down to the road just in time to get a faceful of buckshot from Squat Jensen, him and Big Bob having just arrived.

That left one. He threw away his gun belt, raised his arms, dropped to his knees, and set about the job of begging for his life.

It was Pug Klavinsky.

CHAPTER 23

"Honor and custom dictate that I cannot eliminate him." Pepe laid down his rifle. "But if you should care to...?"

Down below, Big Bob and Squat Jensen had climbed up the rocks and surrounded Pug between the two of 'em.

"I don't guess I'll do that just this minute," I said. "But I'll warn you: that one is the Mange walking on two legs, and he's practiced up on every trick in every book in every language."

"You counsel that his future is to be secured and closely observed?"

"Only just till we hang him. After that, maybe you can let down your guard some."

Sure enough, by the time me and Pepe climbed down, gathered our horses and made our way around to the road, Pug Klavinsky was wrist-tied, neck-roped and standing straight as he could on a wagon bed full of Chinese Bones, parked under the tallest tree for a mile in any direction, and telling the world his opinions about it.

"You can't just hang a man without trial."

"Guess I've heard that one before," Jensen spat on the ground by way of comment. "Try another one and see if it gets a better laugh."

"It ain't legal. Do this and you'll get strung up your own selves."

"I would express myself on the subject at some length," Pepe looked at Klavinsky like something he'd walk around so as not to step in it. "As I was unfortunate to discover the remains of a driver less fortunate than I. But diatribe would only prolong the life of vermin." His lip curled. "*Adios!*"

"I'm saying you can't hang a man just for trying to rob you, nor for a murder I never done. You can't!"

"They can, they will, and they're a-gonna do just that."

I said before how Harve's got a way of just dropping out of the picture without nobody noticing nor remarking on it. Well, he's got the same way of coming back into the picture too, and as he swung off his horse and stepped onto the wagon bed, it was like he'd been here the whole time.

He walked up close to Pug, and spoke soft. "Let me just see if I can explain it to you, because I hate to see a man die ignorant."

He went on, not talking any louder, but there was something in his voice like a judge throwing sentence on a condemned man. Which I guess was the case.

"Pug, maybe you killed that man-- killed him and took his head off just to lay it in the road." He put a hand on Pug's shoulder. "Or maybe you just rode with them as did that deed.

But whichever the case, your friends are gone now and left you to pay the bill. And it's going to be a steep one."

"I'm telling you, we didn't do any of it."

"And I'm telling *you* that no one's ever going to believe that, Pug." The Devil talked like a man does to gentle down a skittish horse or a barking dog. "Don't you see that? You've just got to hang, and these men are going to see it gets done soon and sudden. And that's not all they're going to do."

"It ain't?"

"Nossir, not by a long chalk. When it's over, they won't cut you down. They're going to collect up your dead friends up in the rocks there, and hang them right along beside you."

Pug looked at Harvey for a long time, and it was like some understanding passed between them. He come out with a long, easy sigh. "I guess I understand." He nodded over at Big Bob, tying the loose end of the rope to the base of the tree. "Just doing his job."

"The which is to discourage that sort of thing." Bob readied the reins, and I thought Harvey'd make ready to climb down, but he just stood there next to Pug. Pug looked at him again, and it was kind of different, that look, like he saw something he'd never seen nor thought of before.

"You *know!*" He talked so low I barely heard him say it. "You know we didn't kill that driver. You *know* it… Don't that beat all-llllghch!"

Big Bob had drove the wagon out from under him.

CHAPTER 24

We all stood kind of quiet a spell, while Pug Klavinsky kicked and gurgled and turned purple. Probably it wasn't all that long, but it surely seemed like it. Eventual-like, he finally quit acting up like that, and when he was through, Big Bob turned around in the wagon seat and took a long look at the Devil.

"Just what in tunket were you doing on that dead man's ride anyhow?"

"Nothing much," Harvey shrugged. "Thought I'd side with him there at the end. Let him know he's not alone." He scratched his cheek thoughtfully and climbed down off the wagon. "He was a sorry excuse for a man, wasn't he though?"

"I'd say he was if you hadn't."

"And I'd say it if Bob didn't," I put in. "He'd sell his own mother to Comanches if the price was right."

"Yup." Harvey nodded. "A man like that doesn't get much love in his life. Most likely on account of he doesn't deserve any. I just wanted to give him that little bit to remember while he's burning in Hell."

"Beats the tar out of me." Big Bob shook his head. "But I got a business to run and no time for discussion, which I don't want to make with you anyhow." He turned to me. "Streak, there's two jobs to get done: Moving this load and decorating the trees with those other five crow-baits. I'll give you druthers: Would you druther help with the stringing up and then have me to drive the wagon? Or leave now and handle the team yourself?"

It was decent of Big Bob to give me a choice like that, even if it wasn't really no choice at all. I got no taste in me for hanging up dead men. Come close to losing my breakfast just thinking on it. A thing like that, it'd be a long step down a road I didn't want to walk. And besides that, dead men is heavy.

But I had no notion what-come-ever about handling a six-horse team, so I helped out with the hanging-up whilst Squat Jensen fetched up a board and some paint so Big Bob could make a sign:

THEY KILLED A FARGO DRIVER
Don't you go trying it

Which is how me and Harvey come to be riding alongside the rig and Big Bob driving.

We'd done us a few hours on the trail with maybe some more hours to go between us and Retrospect, when Bob pulled the reins back and stopped close by some good-sized boulders.

"Reckon I'll just step behind them rocks and set a spell." He pulled a big old cotton-pickers' bag out of the wagon bed and trotted off behind the rocks.

Pepe, he'd tied off his horse to the tailgate and fell asleep riding the crates in the wagon bed, and he half-woke in time to see Bob dragging that big sack around to the far side of all this.

"*El Patron*..." he yawned, "He departs our companionship?"

"He'll be back 'fore too long. Just doing his business back there."

Pepe got a puzzled look on him. "Does he harbor ambitions of filling the sack?"

Okay, yeah, we'd spent the morning killing a half-dozen men and posting their dead bodies as a warning, but that pulled a laugh out of me. A good long one, and when it was through, I said, "Well I've heard stories, and knowing Big Bob like I do, I don't doubt he could do it, but he uses that bag to carry his accommodation."

"I must flaunt my ignorance of this accommodation."

"It's kind of a fold-up chair with a hole in it. Big Bob says a man his size likes to set in comfort, times like this. Get him to show it to you sometime."

But he'd already fallen back asleep. Harvey turned to me and commented, "*Señor* Avocado surely seems the capable sort, doesn't he?"

"Cool about it, too. Hang a man, then sleep like an old dog by the hearth."

"Yeah, too bad about him and that woman."

"You saw it too? The way she looked at him like he didn't matter much? How she seen him go off to get in a shooting scrape without even a fare-thee-well? How she—"

"Yeah, I'm old but I don't miss much. Take a look up yonder."

Harvey pointed off to a speck in the distance, up the road a mile or more. Too far off to see much, but looked to me like two riders coming our way, open and friendly-like.

"What do you make of it, Streak?"

"They look peaceable enough, Harve," I squinted hard but it warn't any use. "But I'm just wondering…"

"What you wondering on?"

I looked the Devil straight-on but casual-like. "There was six men, six men and all of 'em pretty hairy, six of 'em, set out to take that wagon."

"And so?"

I went on thinking out loud, but trying to study his face and not look like I was doing it. "There never was a stagecoach carried payload enough to split six ways worth the effort."

"And so?"

"I'm thinking those six were hired for the job of taking that there book, and whoever signed 'em on didn't trust them as far as the next town, so they'd show up somewhere on the road to Retrospect to finish their business. And this here could be them." I cocked another look at--

"Will you, for love or mercy, quit please quit reading my face?"

"Sorry, Harve."

"It's okay." He shrugged. "If you want to know something, just ask me. I don't usually take any fee for answers."

"I just don't like—"

"I know. You don't like to owe me favors."

"I just don't like being beholden." It struck me funny all to once. "Especially when I don't need to be."

"Oh yeah?"

"I mean if you weren't such a misery of a poker player, I wouldn't of picked up the habit."

"That why you quit playing?"

"More like I quit taking candy from a baby. You're just too honest for the game. Shows in your face."

"I'll take that as a compliment."

"Speaking of which… just wanted to tell you that was a fine piece of kindness you did for that never-was-no-good Klavinsky."

"Then give me a smoke on it, Pardner." Harvey reached over and took the makings from my shirt pocket and made himself a smoke. Took a deep pull on it before he turned back to me. "You think that was an act of kindness?"

"Warn't it?"

"I don't know; maybe so. Wasn't meant to be."

"No?"

"Nossir." He took another deep pull and turned it into a smoke ring. "I just figured Hell's going to mean a lot more to old Pug now that he knows how much sweeter things could have been right here."

"Harvey? You did that just out of meanness?"

"Not meanness quite exactly. I enjoy a good joke, that's all."

There's sometimes I forget Harvey's the Devil. Sometimes I wonder is he really pure Evil like they say.

And there's sometimes I don't wonder at all.

Big Bob finished his business and dragged his bag out from behind the rock just then. "What's your talking?" In the back of the wagon, Pepe stirred, yawned, and almost woke up but decided against it. Big Bob grinned. "Must have been almighty interesting."

"Just discussing the late Pug Klavinsky," Harvey said.

I took a squint at the two riders coming our way so slow and easy, and now that I could see them some better, they put me in mind of a picture I saw once in a book called DON QUIXOTE. There's these two riders, one of 'em's tall and gawky, the other's short and round. Still couldn't see much of the two coming our way, but they looked some like that.

Banneker was facing the same direction and squinting his eyes near-shut. "Anybody got a pair of field glasses?"

"I never feel the need to look that close," Harvey said, "Seems like most everything comes to me, sooner or later. "

At about which time Pepe Avocado finally sat himself up. "*Yo me despierto.* I awaken. What transpires?"

Bob left off squinting. "Just wishing I had me some binoculars to get a closer-up look at them two coming this way."

"Why for you want that?" I asked.

"On account of they got a pair looking at us. Just saw another flash off it."

He was right. And now that I looked at the short one, I saw he wasn't so much short and fat as he was stocky and square-built. And the tall one, he wasn't just gawky; there was something clear wrong with how he moved his head.

"You reckon they got anything to do with the bunch we just strung?"

"Most likely they don't ..." Big Bob rubbed his jaw thoughtful-like. "On the other hand, wouldn't shock me none if they were. Too bad we can't ask any of them dead ones."

"Looks like the live ones'll be close enough pretty soon that you can ask straight out yourselves." Harvey said.

"*Señor* Harvey," Pepe was full awake now. "I observed the man we hanged, him in conversation with you, prior to his demise. Did he perhaps divulge information of pertinence?"

"He said he and the men we shot it out with never chopped off that head and left it in the road."

"So he spoke falsehoods right up to his ending." Pepe spat in disgust.

"Nossir," Harvey shook his head sadly. "He did not."

"You're loco." Bob got to looking kind of peevish. I said before how he never liked the Devil very much, and he wasn't about to hear him out patiently. "If they didn't do it, then who in purple mountain's majesty did?"

"My guess is it would be one—maybe both—of those gentlemen just now coming up on us with artillery showing."

CHAPTER 25

"He's quite correct." The voice came out of the tall man all smooth, deep, and practiced as a preacher on Sunday.

Two men. Two horses. Two shotguns suddenly pulled fast and close and pointed our way.

I've had some tough cusses level their sights in my direction. And I'll confess, it upsets me some. But there was something else, something different about these two. I could feel it like a cold wind.

But Big Bob Banneker, he just smiled and come out with, "I'm surmising you must be Headless Hinchley!"

I could see pretty evident that the deep-voiced man, he didn't like being called that, and I could see even plainer why he got the name. He wore a stiff leather collar tight around his neck, but his head wobbled and twisted when he moved, like it was near to coming off. I'd heard talk around him here and elsewhere. Suspicious talk it was, but nothing recent, and nothing ever proved of it. Now I looked him all over and wondered about some of that talk.

There was something or other riding with him, too. Some critter I seen pictures of on the walls at Sheriff's offices. Short and hairy it was, wearing a bear-skin, or at leastways I think so. Plain fact of it was that I couldn't tell for sure where the bear-skin left off and his own hide took up. Anyways, he had him a short, nasty-looking sword stuck in his belt, which was his signature, and the posters called him Slasher Jim Trask.

But there was more to 'em. I couldn't put my finger right on it, and it's not easy to explain, but bad as they were individually, there was something about the two of them, paired together, something *between* them, and it like to set my teeth on edge.

Big Bob ignored it. "Streak my boy, let me introduce you to Headless Hinchley."

My eyes moved from his gun to his face.

"We've met," I said.

"I don't recall it."

"You wouldn't. You did me a kindness then."

"I'll do you another one now. I'm going to allow you gentlemen to throw down your guns and live a short while longer."

"I express abundant gratitude to you for such generosity." Pepe jumped down off the cart beside of me, reached up his left hand and took his hat off in the wide, courteous gesture of a Spanish *grandee*. "However, I am not inclined to so accept. Perhaps you may ponder over your unwise offer."

"The offer stands." Hinchley near-smiled, "But not much longer."

"The Mexican's got a point, Mister Hinchley," Big Bob said, "You two look awful outnumbered from where I'm standing."

"We have guns out."

"And we could too, if we wanted a lot of killin'. Hell, I reckon *Señor* Avocado's got his'n out already. Did you notice he took off his hat lefty-handed?"

I seen it myself. Pepe was holding his hat at his waist now, and that wide brim covered his gunbelt and his right hand both.

"You impair my renown, *Señor* Banneker." He put on a hurt look. "I aspire to such courtesy in manner merely to inculcate seeds of doubt in the headless one."

I looked to see how Hinchley was taking this, and for a moment, it was like a cloud must of went by overhead, and a shadow passed across his face. But then it moved on, and I could see his expression hadn't changed at all, like a face on a statue.

"Keep him guessing, Pepe." I said.

"You gentlemen seem tired of living." Hinchley's voice was steady as ever, same as his face. "Or perhaps you overestimate my patience."

Big Bob glanced at me and Pepe both, a look that said *Let me do the talking* and he turned back to Hinchley.

"Okay, Slick, you got the drop on us, but it ain't such an almighty edge, is it? Any shooting starts, well tote up the figures: there's two of you, and you got four guns to aim at; there's four of us—"

"Beg pardon?" Harvey asked in a low tone, "You want me on your team now, do you Bob?"

"Get thee behind me," Big Bob dropped his voice a few notches and snarled back at him in a whisper. Not sure how he did it exactly, but I'll swear I heard him snarl in a whisper, without taking his eyes off Hinchley or Trask. He raised his voice again.

"I say there's four of us here that might get a notion to draw and aim at just two of you. And one of us is Streak Wilson there."

"Almighty thanks for putting the cross-hairs on me like that, Bob."

"Don't mention it, Streak." Bob kept his eyes front, still talking to them other two. "What do you say to that?"

Slasher Jim Trask made some kind of noise that rumbled out of his hairy chest like a big hungry critter in a deep cave. Hinchley moved his lips into something like a smile.

"I believe we may be harder to put down than you seem to think."

"Slasher Jim? That's as things may go. But *you* surely won't be much trouble." Big Bob gave out what I read about in books, where they call it a mirthless laugh. It's like a regular laugh, only there ain't any fun in it. "Hell, if any shooting starts, I'd wager the recoil off that 12-gauge'll knock you clean off your saddle and halfway back to Retrospect."

"Your charm wears thin, Mister Banneker, and your time runs short. Give up your guns."

"C'mon now, Hinchley, you don't want our guns. You didn't send six men after us to get our guns, now didja? I'm of the opinion you'd much rather have what we got in the wagon here, am I right?"

"Time is fleeting, Mister Banneker."

"Well take the damn thing. Ain't nothing in it worth killing a man over."

That raised eyebrows on Trask. At least I think they were eyebrows; looked so much like the rest of him, I wasn't sure. Hinchley reached up a hand to his chin and kind of pointed his face at Big Bob.

"You're surrendering a Fargo load?"

"Under certain conditions, I am."

"You're making conditions now?"

"And if you're smart, you'll be taking them."

Pepe sidled up close to my horse and tugged my boot strap. "Your pardon, *Señor* Wilson," He kept his voice low. "I grow disoriented. Is this to be a robbery, or a transaction of commerce?"

"You remember what I said about a man who'll fight when he has to, but he'd rather not?" I whispered back. He nodded. "Well, watch this one."

Big Bob was talking. "...Think there's something in there you want. I say there ain't, but I'm not going to argue it with you. So if I let you take this load without a fight, I want your word you won't tear up what's in there, and you'll leave it close by the Fargo office in Retrospect."

"You'll trust me for that?"

"I don't trust you any farther than I can see a gnat in a rainstorm. You'll have to post a cash bond for that wagon and contents."

Slasher Jim made another low, angry noise deep in his throat. Sounded like "Gonna kill'im." I spent a half-second on studying him and that sword he always wore: short, sharp, wide, and heavy-looking, just like the man who carried it, and probably just as unpleasant close-up.

Only he wouldn't carry something like that unless he'd rather chop up a man close-to than shoot him down from any distance away. That's a bad one all right, but there's more to it than that:

If a man carries a sword, then he doesn't use a gun much, and straight-shooting isn't a thing you want to do second-best, So if I was playing with the odds and had to decide who to shoot first...

Hinchley made a motion like he was holding the other guy back. I thought at the time he must be calculating his chances if any shooting started, and not liking them much, and I guessed he didn't know they'd just got a lot shorter.

"Cash bond?" he snorted, "Mister Banneker, you seem prone to hallucination. I suggest you cool your fevered brow with a damp kerchief and rest in the shade until it passes."

"Are you saying No?"

"You perceive correctly, Sir."

"Well, I got to have something for security. Give me your horse."

That's when things turned bad.

I don't know why, and I'm not sure how I knew it, but I caught the look in Hinchley's eyes and thought to myself, *Keep it up, Bob, and you won't have to worry over any horse—six of your friends going to carry you there by the handles if you don't stop riling this broke-necked killer.* I moved closer to my saddle gun.

Hinchley pretended not to see it, but Trask served me a look that would've shamed a skunk. I gave them both back a steady stare that said I was trying to decide which one to kill first.

The mood here had changed all right.

I felt it again, that wave of some funny kind of energy betwixt Hinchley and Trask. But if Big Bob noticed, he didn't let on. "Just look at the wagon I'm trusting you with…" He moved to the side and slapped a wheel. "Solid oak and fresh steel tires on each one. What do you say?"

"I say my horse alone is worth more than that wagon, the nags pulling it, and the peasant trying to sell it to me."

"Oh, this ain't selling, Hinch." Big Bob ran his hand alongside the wagon bed, back to the rear wheel. "We're just talking toward security posted for the wagon and contents, all of which are to be returned in good working order. Now as to your horse… Mmmmm… I guess I could throw in fifty dollars for the saddle. What do you say?"

"I say this is a hundred-dollar saddle, which money your heirs and assigns shall shortly need for your funeral expenses. Do you understand me, sir?"

"If you paid a hundred for that rig, you must have been drunk at the time. I can go as high as seventy-five if the boys here will chip in and—" He moved back to us and took off his hat like he was collecting for a church-raising. "—and Streak, you toss your side-arm here, then start shooting, boys, 'cause this is the best chance we'll get today."

I said a little ways back about how Pepe Avocado had tied off his horse to the back of the wagon. Well, Big Bob had maneuvered back thataways, still talking, and when he said that part about *this is the best chance we'll get today* he fanned his hat in that horse's face, and the horse reared up and went crazy, jumping, snorting, rearing, bucking... and while he's doing all that, Bob slapped his hat back on his head.

And then everything that ever happened in the world came around all at once and happened again, fast and sudden and all over us.

CHAPTER 26

I tossed my hand gun to Big Bob, pulled the Spencer from its saddle scabbard, jacked a round as I raised it to my shoulder, and pitched a shot at Hinchley almost quicker than he could squeeze trigger on his scattergun.

But almost didn't count in this game. Hinchley fired both barrels, and the blast from his gun tore a hole in the wagon gate where Big Bob was standing right when he tried to duck for cover. I didn't see if he made it or didn't; just saw his hat go flying, and I couldn't say was his head still in it or not.

Like I say, I got off a shot at Hinchley, but the recoil from his shotgun done just like Bob said it would: threw Hinchley backwards so hard my round just sailed through the empty air where he'd been taking up space a split-second ago.

I wasn't looking that way anymore anyhow. I turned in the saddle and got a shot off at Slasher Jim just as he raised his shotgun, and my round meant for his lungs shattered the stock on his twin-barrel before he could fire.

Yeah, but it went off anyway. Tore up a lot of dirt and singed the mane on his horse. That poor animal let out a howl that'll haunt me to my dying day, and then set to jumping, and then into a charge straight at us.

Didn't throw Slasher Jim, though. He just squeezed his legs to hang on, pulled the cutlass from his belt and come hacking and swinging right in amongst us.

Well, Damn.

Wasn't much any of us could do about that except get out of his way, or try to. Even close up, I wouldn't risk a shot at a target moving in and out of between and around the rest of us. Bob came out from under the wagon shooting, stopped to pick his target, and almost lost his head for the second time in as many minutes when Slasher Jim Trask come up alongside him and swung that awful blade down on Bob's neck, just when Pepe got off a shot that missed Slasher Jim's shoulder and zinged past my head way too close. Spoiled Trask's swing, though, long enough for Bob to reconsider himself back under the wagon. For a minute or two the whole scene was just a circus in Hell, what with Pepe and Big Bob ducking, darting and dodging every which-of-a-way, the wagon team straining to bolt with the brake set, and Bucky having fits under my butt.

Then Big Bob yelled, "Pull yerselves back!" I reined Bucky around and rode clear of the whole runction the same time Pepe come running, and I almost trampled Bob in the confusion, but the three of us got clear to where we could group up and all of us get a respectable shot at whatever there was that needed one.

Just in time to see Slasher Jim Trask jump on the wagon, grab the reins, and free the brake.

That wagon team went clear crazy, careening off the trail, then back, pulling Pepe's horse behind 'em, and before it could pick up any speed, Hinchley threw himself up and on board, his head flopping around like a Christmas goose

And off they went.

"Looks to me like old Slasher Jim knows how to move a six-horse team." Big Bob got off a shot that I swore must have hit Trask or Hinchley, one or the other, but it didn't slow 'em up any at all. Bob lowered his gun again.

"They're got away and gone."

CHAPTER 27

I could of took a shot at them myself, but Bucky was still hopping, start-stopping, and generally making a commotion under me so's if I tried, I could be sure of hitting sky or ground, but not much else.

It was too late anyhow. Nothing to do but watch that Fargo wagon lose itself in a cloud of dust, and start counting our arms and legs.

Sum total we came up with was that Big Bob had caught buckshot across his back—deep enough to ruin his coat, but not his skin very much—whilst Pepe's wide-brim hat now looked more like an open-top chimney, and Bucky had some ways collected a round of double-aught buckshot square in the saddle-bag, halfway through my copy of THE MOONSTONE.

"It is opportune that you opted for such a weighty tome," Pepe surveyed the damage with me. "Lighter fare might have resulted in injury to your equine."

"To blazes with that horse." Big Bob craned himself around and stared down at his torn coat tails. "I come near to getting my butt blistered, and out here in this country, that's as good as dead. Speaking of which—" He eyed me close. "Did I hear you say as how you knew Headless Hinchley?"

"Seems I recollect it. Pretty sure, anyhow."

So I told them about how I joined up with the Confederate Army just because my dad died fighting for the South. I was young then, just a kid, but I was also big for my age, and they weren't choosy. And I lasted just long enough to charge across an open field into a volley of Yankee cannon-fire.

"Next thing I know, it's night time and I'm lying on the ground with the awfullest pain in my head I ever felt, and hope I never feel again. Then this tall, skinny man, he's sneaking around, taking what he can off the bodies—mostly Yankee bodies, because we Rebs didn't have much of nothing to steal."

"A despoiler of deceased combatants," Pepe gasped.

"You mean a battlefield ghoul," Big Bob snorted.

"I think it was him, anyhow. Never knew his right name, of course. But he pulled a hunk of metal out of my head, put a blue uniform shirt on me, and dragged me back into the Yankee camp."

Big Bob rubbed his chin, thoughtful-like. "Probably thought he'd use you to make his way out without getting caught."

"That's as may be, but he saved my life, and they got him anyhow. Leastways, I think they did. I wasn't right in the head for a long ways after, but I kind of remember me laying on a cot and seeing them march him off to hang him from a wagon tongue. Could be I just dreamed that, but I don't think so."

"It'd account for his head wobbling around like it does."

"That which you say is indubitable," Pepe said, "In my studies I have read of men executed yet not deceased."

"Chills my soul just to think on it," the Devil said.

I looked over at Harvey sitting his horse right here amongst us, kind of startled to see him turn up so sudden like he did. But nobody else seemed like they'd even noticed him gone.

"Seems to me you gentlemen at least show a talent for staying out of harm's way." Harvey grinned down from his saddle. "Yessir, and it's a good job you did of it too."

I already said how Big Bob never cared much for the Devil, and right now his blood was up from shooting and getting shot at, so I guess there's no wonder he acted like he did. He took Harvey's comment like a personal face-slapping, and when he turned to answer, there was plain murder in his eye.

So there was going to be a fight:

Big Bob Banneker,
Wells Fargo's Curly Wolf
(west of the Mississippi)
}up against{
Harvey Rideout,
(Prince of Darkness.)

I'd have put up even money either way.
And I would have lost.

CHAPTER 28

What came next wasn't a fight; it was a beating. But a beating like nothing I ever saw before, a thing I still look back on and wonder about.

Big Bob stalked over to Harvey sitting up there on his horse, and he reached up, grabbed him by the belt and jerked him down to the ground so hard it raised dust. Then he up and kicked Harvey in the ribs, and I swear I heard bones break.

Harvey, he just got up easy as you please, not a mark on him, and stood there looking patient.

I don't think Big Bob noticed anything wrong; he was that mad. He waded into Harvey with a one-two-three-four in the belly, each one a powerhouse; bent Harvey double-over, and the last one lifted him clean off the ground, only old Harvey never landed down again because Big Bob served him up a pile-drive square in the face that bounced him back off a rock and right into another set of knuckles square in the mouth.

He should have been spitting up blood and choking on his own teeth. But Harvey just got his balance back and stood there like he was bored with waiting.

Bob saw it. Saw how blows that rightly should of killed a man landed square on Harvey and just never bothered him. And it drove him clear crazy.

He made some kind of noise, somewhere between a wildcat roar and a baby-sob, raging and helpless all to the same time, and he hit old Harvey and he kicked him, and he grabbed him by the neck and slammed his head on the ground, and I don't know what all else, and Pepe stared and gaped and crossed himself, and I heard him squeak "*Madre de Dios!*"

I couldn't of said it any better myself. I looked at Pepe and he looked at me, and the two of us moved in and you'd think we should of pulled Big Bob off of Harvey before he done himself harm trying to kill the Devil. But we done no sort of thing as that.

Instead, we made like we was holding down Harvey, pinning him to the ground, and in a second or two, It finally dawned on old Bob that the fight was over.

He leaned up against my horse, shook his head, wiped sweat from his eyes, and muttered, "Where the hell was I?"

"You just stepped out of your head for a mite, that's all."

Harvey walked away to collect his horse. Bob looked at him like he'd made up his mind over something, but I couldn't tell what. "Well, I'm back at home now, thank you."

"The exercise was an honor," Pepe kept his voice low and soothing. "I express my appreciation to you for it. And behold!"

Harvey came back leading Pepe's horse, and them which Hinchley and Trask came in on had followed back our way and took to sniffing at Bucky's feed bag.

"So we've got back to where I was trying to get us with all that talk." Big Bob looked crossways at the Devil and shook his head. "Now let's check the cargo."

He fetched up the cotton-picking bag, pulled his seat out of it, and reached down in again.

And came out with a crate. Maybe a yard square and half a yard deep.

"You were right about it, Streak." He picked up the crate one-handed and set it on a good-sized rock. "Worth all the toil of digging it out from under all those crates of Heathen bones. And pretty near worth the work of strapping the load down again."

"Don't tell me you done the strapping, Bob."

"No, but I had to listen to Squat Jensen belly-ache all over it."

"You're a tough one."

He stuck his hand back down in the bag and came up with a steel hatchet.

"And I'm aiming to see what all the fuss is about."

CHAPTER 29

I sure never thought I'd see the day Big Bob Banneker would stick his fingers in another man's business, much less hack into it with a hand-axe. That's what he done, though; split that crate with one hatchet-stroke at the edge and pulled out whatever-it-was.

I took it for a slab of wood at first, it was that solid-heavy. Then I saw hinges at one side, big silver ones, and a shiny knob on top, so I reckoned it must be some kind of box, or maybe a trunk for stowing really short stuff. But when I got a close look at the sides, I finally saw it wasn't a solid piece of wood, nor a box neither; the sides was the edges of pages, and this thing was a book.

Big Bob set it down on a flat rock—the one he bounced Harvey off of—and I'm saying it wasn't like any book I ever saw before or since. The covers were polished hardwood, the binding was bolted and plated...

I caught Harvey watching me, and he had a funny look on him. "What do you make of it, Streak?'

"How's a man supposed to read this beast?"

"With all due deliberation, *Señor* Wilson," Pepe sounded like a gunsmith teaching how to take a Winchester apart and put it back together right. "With expertise in the handling, respect in the use, and though it be spurious blasphemy, a certain reverence in merely beholding it."

He looked down at the book, then over at Big Bob. "*Con su permiso?*"

"Go right ahead, *Señor*." Bob near bowed, he was that gracious.

Pepe put on a pair of thin white gloves and ran a hand gently across the wooden cover, then sniffed the glove. He looked close at the hinges and the bolts that held them on. Fingered the edges and the decoration on top that I thought was a handle at first, that's how big it was. Finally, he turned to Big Bob.

"Please to position yourself over there, that you may intercept the sunlight in *sombra*?"

Harvey grinned wide while Bob moved into place, but Pepe waited till that book was full-covered with shadow, and when he was satisfied it was, he opened it up real slow, listening, smelling, and squinting close all to the same time.

Then, using his long, delicate fingers like tweezers, he turned a single page and brushed his pinky finger lightly across a line or so of the writing. He looked at his glove, took it off, and ran the same finger over another line. He pulled a lens out of his pocket and looked at the writing so close his nose near touched the page.

Finally, he straightened up. The look on his face, I don't know how to say it, but it's like he was saying goodbye to someone he loved, someone he'd always love...

"She is deceit," he sighed. "Executed with the intimacy of a master craftsman, perforce an artist of profound adulation for such vocation. I should say no more than two centuries overly tardy."

"Do tell."

Pepe pitched a sharp look at me. "You discredit my credibility?"

"No, I'm just trying to figure out what you said."

"You're saying this-here's forged?" Big Bob looked down at the book-or-whatever-it-was, and up at Pepe.

"In my opinion, this is necessarily such event."

"Well, why the wherefore?"

"Figured you'd spot it," Harve' winked at Pepe. "What tipped you to it?"

"It totals the accumulation of factors contributing." Pepe looked at Harvey like he was glad to have an audience. "The Grand Grimoire was written—"

"The Grand Who?" Bob interrupted.

Pepe nodded to Harvey, "Perhaps you should to elucidate."

"A Grimoire is a book of spells, curses, or incantations," Harvey said, "The name comes from the French word for Grammar, and it'd take too long to tell how it came to be applied to the ersatz opus in front of us. Am I right so far, *Señor* Avocado?"

Pepe nodded and Harvey went on, "So they call this one the Grand Grimoire—"

"On occasion, it is nomenclatured as The Red Dragon or Satan's Bible," Pepe put in.

"Attributed to Satan, but authorship has never been firmly established." Harvey chuckled. "One story is that it was originally written in Aramaic by old King Solomon, but the only copies anyone's ever seen are Latin translations, done by Monks along about six hundred years ago."

"What's it about and who's in the story?" Bob asked.

"There is no story," Pepe said, "It is in the genre of non-fiction, a book of instruction and guidance in the summoning of demons."

"What for would a man want demons around?"

"I am concerned only with the book itself," Pepe said, "The book as an object. To be examined, observed, and analyzed, certainly. But decidedly perhaps not to be utilized."

Big Bob turned to Harvey. "Well, Mister Rideout, seeing as how you're in a position to know, maybe you can explain it to me." Funny how he said that, in a voice like he was joking, only he wasn't really. And when Harvey answered, he talked just as light-but-serious.

"According to that book there, when you summon up a demon, imp, succubus or whichever, and do it right… well, that critter has to take its marching orders from you. Only you have to be careful—awful careful—to handle it just right." He turned to me. "Don'cha Streak?"

I dodged the question. "Pepe, you say that book there ain't the real goods?"

"Regrettably so," Pepe gave it that lost-love look of his again. "Observe, gentlemen…" Bob and I closed in on him whilst he held a magnifier-glass. "The cross bar on this 'T'"

That writing was more made for prettiness than for reading, but I managed to find what he was talking about.

"Looks okay to me."

"Observe with excessive closeliness the pattern left by the brush in ink… do you detect it?"

"I see it." Big Bob wiped his eyes from the strain "What's so special about it?"

"In which direction was the pen moving when it made this mark?"

I looked at it closer. "Seems like the line is a little heavier, sharper, on the right side."

"I see what you mean, Streak," Big Bob nodded. "So that'd mean… Lessee… I'd say the pen was moving from right to left when it made that mark."

"You determine it with precision." Pepe said, "The natural way of one employing the left hand."

"So?"

"In the Monasteries where such things were reduplicated and preserved, the Monks were admissible to utilize only the right hand in their work. It follows then that this was not produced in those circumstances and is hence spurious."

"Doggers!" Big Bob shook his head in wonderment. "You got all that from a line half-a-inch long?"

"Other attenuating factors remain extant," Pepe leafed carefully through the pages while he talked, "The paper, the oil used to polish the cover, the ink... All would have been available, yet rarefied during the period of—Oh my!" He bent closer and peered down, like he was reading real careful. "This arouses studiousness."

"You see more of those funny lines?" I asked.

"This is deviation. Not of calligraphy but of nomenclature." He could see I was getting lost in his dust, so he slowed it down for me. "The Grand Grimoire is defined as a book of spells for calling up Satan and his emissaries: Lucifer, Beelzebub, Mephistopheles... But this—" He got a look on his face like a man getting ready to lift a heavy load, then set about explaining:

"The mythology of ancient times is known to you? The Gods and Goddesses? Aphrodite? Zeus? Apollo? Thor, Odin, Freya?"

"I read a book of stories about 'em." It was good reading, too.

"They named the days and months after some of them, didn't they?" Big Bob put in.

"Excellent. Thus, we have foundation for explanation." Pepe relaxed to see this wasn't going to be too big of a chore. "These legends partake similarities, and disparities as well, such as..." He looked to gauge his students' attention span and skipped ahead. "Yet each and all of them refer to a pre-dynasty of Deities, traversing a universe before Earth has been created, totally diverse from the idea of our Christian God or even the pagan divinities of ancient times."

"You mean like back then, someone maybe asked Where did Zeus come from? and this was the answer?"

"Excessively similar." Pepe gave me A for Effort. "Yet these deities of the pre-mythology were not remotely like us. Nor like any god we could imagine. They were formless creatures in a chaotic universe. Cannibals. Eaters of their own spawn— of their own parents!—beings not of creation, but destruction for self-preservation: Ouranous, Gaia, Kronos, Chaos, gods of super power, in constant conflict, eternal turmoil, desperately clinging to their own existence by obliteration and holocaust."

He took him a deep breath. "Yet each one of them was supplanted, flushed into some dark, eternal limbo as a Universe was formed, and then Earth, and other gods supplanted them, and were in turn supplanted by a God of goodness and light."

"This calls them back."

He leafed a few pages more. "And this…" He cleared his throat and shut the book.

"It encompasses an incantation for returning the dead to living form."

CHAPTER 30

"If you say so," Bob sounded like he'd got hold of about half of what Pepe was saying and was still rassling with the rest. I wondered who'd win. He turned to me.

"Now as for you, Mister Streak Wilson, I got two things to say: First, I'm glad you came along for this job. Glad it was you and Pepe up there in those rocks, doing the hard work. I've been glad of you before this, too. A dozen nights or more I've slept better knowing you were taking care of things. I can't say it good enough, and I should have said it more often, but there it is. You're a good man and I'm proud to have known you."

"Come to that, Big Bob, you're a good man to work for."

"Not any more I'm not."

"Howzat?"

"You're fired."

"Come again?"

"You can draw your wages and a bonus from the Fargo office in Retrospect tomorrow. It's been nice knowing you, but no man who rides with this—" He pointed at Harvey and took a second to hunt up the right word. "No man who rides with this one is going to work for me."

Pepe looked back and forth from me to Big Bob and back again, then over at Harvey. "Comprehension fails me, Señor Banneker. You sever the employment of an estimable individual because of this maleficent one?"

"I'm not going to discuss it."

"Makes me all over rueful," Harvey said it like he meant it. "To cost a man his job, just for befriending—"

"I said I'm not discussing it." Big Bob served me a look like a door slamming shut. "Goodbye, Streak. Gonna miss you."

I didn't answer him.

Couldn't.

Just got up on Bucky and rode on out of there, off the main trail, and down the Confluence Cut-Off, with Harvey almost alongside.

But me riding just ahead so's he wouldn't see me crying.

CHAPTER 31

"Now you take those first three Commandments," the Devil was saying, "And mind you, these are the ones at the top of the list, ahead of cheating, lying, stealing… even killing a man. And they are as follows: *I am the Lord thy God, thou shalt have no other Gods but me; Thou shalt not take My Name in vain;* and *Thou shalt keep the Sabbath Day holy.*"

"Never thought about it, but I guess that's right. And so?"

"Doesn't all that sound just a little needy?"

"Put it that way… Like I said, I guess I just hadn't given it much thought. You sure those are the very first three?"

"Those and none other, Pard'. Guess I ought to know my Bible."

We'd eaten up the rest of the day riding a trail they call the Confluence Cut-Off, on account of it's shorter than the main road to Retrospect. Not faster, though. Three good-sized creeks meet up there, and the land around them goes from hilly to near-mountainous, so you got to weave back and forth, up and down, sideways and widdershins, to get through it. And the creeks I told about, you get a hard rain and they just ain't safe to cross.

We were riding alongside one of those creeks now, looking for a safe fording, and Harvey looked mighty doubtful about it.

"I guess we came this way because you want to put some time and space betwixt yourself and Mister Banneker."

"I'm trying to figure out why I feel so damn bad on it." I saw a shallow spot with a rocky bed and urged Bucky into the stream. The rush of the water drowned out talk till we got across. "I fully meant to quit Wells Fargo just as soon as I put the quietus on Pug Klavinsky anyhow."

"And now that's over and done to a fare-thee-dead."

"So I should ought to of been glad old Bob saved me the work of quitting."

The rocky creek bank made for tricky going, but better than getting stuck in soft mud. We gave our mounts their own heads as we went, they were smart enough to find sound footing, and as we picked our way along, Harvey observed, "Somehow, you don't look real glad over it, though."

"I'm a long ways from that."

"And mostly my fault." Harvey dismounted to get Tennessee up a steep slope. I did likewise, and neither of us said anything till we'd wrestled our horses to the crest, where things flattened out and the regular road into Retrospect stretched out ahead of us.

I got my breath back and said, "More like the fault of those jaspers that killed a man trying to steal a worthless book."

"Worthless?"

"Pepe showed how he knew it was forged. Wasn't you listening?"

"And you believed him?"

"Didn't you?"

"I wouldn't give odds on it, no."

"What about that line he showed us, the one that went right to left, but the monks only used their right hand…"

"That line and a thousand more like it only make it more likely that book is genuine."

"How you figure?"

"Those Monks kept history and literature alive for a thousand years and more, copying words out by hand for the glory of God, and a good part of it they didn't understand. Some of it in languages they never learned. Pity there weren't more of 'em. But your friend Pepe kind of overlooked the fact that those holy men would never have copied and preserved anything as purely wicked as the Grand Grimoire. More likely they'd have burned it."

We headed our horses up the road as he went on, "The Grand Grimoire would have been copied by folks set on defying the scriptures. The kind of yahoos that hang crosses upside down and say the Lord's Prayer bass-ackwards, then tell themselves how wicked they be." He spat. "Easy marks. And when pay-back time comes around, they fall on their knees and pray for God to pick up the tab. Not like you."

I made like I didn't catch that last part. "Are you saying that book's the genuine article?"

"I'm not saying it for sure. Just there's no proof it's not."

I could respect the difference. "Well, come down to it, even if that book is real, that don't mean that what's in it is true. Could just be a thousand-year-old lie."

"Or even an ancient misunderstanding, passed down for generations."

I studied the road ahead and the sun above. Looked like they were getting closer together. Might be as late as Six or early as Four. Hard telling, this time of year. By now, Banneker and Pepe must be at least two hours ahead of us. Maybe even made it into Retrospect…

I got to thinking about that book, and how Hinchley and Trask thought they'd got it away from Big Bob. My mind wandered over to what Pepe said about them ancient pre-gods or whatever they were. The ones that disappeared so long ago their shadows was turned to dust, and even the memory of them had dried up and blown away. Good thing, too, from what Pepe said … and there was something else, too. Something else Pepe said, about … something or other…

That's when it hit me. A thought fast and hard and pure awful. Don't know where it came from, nor why, nor how it got there, but it come to me in a flash bright enough to hurt.

"Harvey," I said, "Them two trying to steal that book…"

"What about 'em, Streak?"

"They ain't regular men, are they?"

"That's one way to put it."

"Then they must want that book pretty bad."

"I wouldn't be at all surprised."

"Could be they'll make another try for it."

"That's as may be. You don't work for Fargo or Banneker anymore."

He had a point there.

"No, I surely don't."

"So what's your hurry now?" He'd noticed me clicking up Bucky's pace some.

I didn't answer. Just urged Bucky on a tad faster.

CHAPTER 32

Banneker and Pepe were just outside Retrospect, maybe a half hour left to ride, when they saw the wagon fifty yards ahead.

The empty wagon.

The empty wagon surrounded by broken crates and a hundred scattered bones.

The empty wagon surrounded by scattered bones, and crowned with a beautiful woman sitting regally in the seat.

"*La Dona* Maria!" Pepe put spurs to his horse and sped to the wagon.

"The Heathen Bones!" Banneker took in the scene and processed it swiftly: *Rocks a short ways off… big enough to hide a man… Or two… but too far away for an ambush… Now what's the Queen of Damn-All-Everything doing here?*

He trotted his horse up to the wagon, staring down at the broken crates and jumbled bones that would never get to China.

"Somebody's gonna pay for this," he muttered.

He raised his eyes to the woman in the wagon. "Whatcha doing here, *Señorita?*"

Pepe left off staring at the woman and turned to Banneker. "Some respect, if you please. *La Dona* Maria Sophia Vales is the ward of the late *caballero* Don Marcus de la Manderleros." He took off his hat.

Banneker thought of a good answer, then decided it might get him shot. "I beg your pardon, *Dona* Maria." He uncovered his head politely. "You may understand my surprise at finding you here."

"Did you expect me to sit idly by in that disgusting hovel until another hot and uncomfortable coach arrived to convey my person?"

"Well, Ma'am, I surely didn't look to see you sitting up there in a Bones Wagon. Where's the men that were with it?"

"I cannot say."

"And how did you get here?"

She smiled. It was not a pretty sight. "Your man Wilson traced out the way for me when he circled around the Rock Hills. I simply took a horse and followed his tracks, then continued on toward the town of Retrospect."

Banneker looked around and saw the horse a ways off, idly searching the hard terrain for anything edible.

"Now you will excuse us, as I must speak with this one." *Dona* Maria turned to Pepe.

This one, Banneker thought to himself. *He's stark crazy over her, and she calls him "this one."*

He looked at them carefully. Something in her attitude was wrong: the way she sat half-facing him, the controlled tension in her movements, her tone of voice. This wasn't just indifference, Banneker decided, it was—

"*Querido, destruyete,*" she said softly.

Pepe's eyes widened in shock.

"*Destroy myself? I cannot!*"

He drew his pistol.

"I must proceed to the municipality of Retrospect and disclose my observations on—"

"*Querido, destruyete,*" she repeated. "In the heart. It is fitting."

He put the muzzle to his chest.

"I love you, my Darling." She gazed tenderly into his eyes. "*Querido, destruyete!*"

Pepe shot himself in the heart and fell instantly to the ground.

"Lady--?" Banneker tried to form words to make sense of it. "What just--? What did--?"

"He died thinking I loved him," Maria Sophia said calmly. "It was kind of me."

"And it put you in an advantageous position, my good Banneker." The rich, cultured voice came from behind him. "Now be a smart fellow and disarm yourself before you turn around."

Still dazed by Pepe's sudden death, Big Bob carefully drew the long gun from its saddle scabbard and dropped it. His sidearm followed.

"Now turn around."

He reined his horse around.

Faced Headless Hinchley and Slasher Jim Trask.

They faced him back.

His gaze took in Trask's cutlass, Hinchley's shotgun, and dead Pepe on the ground.

"You got class, Hinchley." He made his voice sound relaxed and conversational. "And a style all your own."

"Thank you, Banneker."

"I see it now. Before you come at a man, you get him stopped, then pull his attention away from you personal, so's he doesn't see you coming till you been there and gone."

"Stage magicians—charlatans—call it misdirection."

"So I reckon it was you that dropped Blondie Ribbins' head on the trail outside East Forks."

Dona Maria shifted impatiently on the wagon seat. Banneker looked at her cautiously.

"I still can't figure how she did that trick with Pepe."

"It wasn't a trick."

"Must have been some kind of mesmerism then. Pretty slick, too."

"Hardly," Hinchley steadied his head. "It requires time and a receptive subject. With you we have neither."

"I gotta see it again. Can she work it on old Slasher Jim here?" He gestured at Trask.

Trask remained impassive. Hinchley almost smiled. *Dona* Maria just looked annoyed. "He wastes our time." She waved a hand disdainfully down at the broken crates and scattered remains.

"Don't blame me for that," Banneker kept his voice even and measured. "I told you there wasn't anything you wanted in that there wagon."

"So you did. And I naturally assumed you were lying."

"Yeah, and I naturally wish you hadn't made such a hash of things." Big Bob looked around at the litter of human remains and shook his head. "Gonna be a lot of heathens awful upset about this."

"Wells Fargo can afford it."

"I'm not talking money. It's religion with them. Like you tore up the family bible or—"

"He wastes our time." *Dona* Maria repeated.

"Do I?"

"Don't you?" Hinchley sounded like he already knew the answer, and Banneker wouldn't like it.

"That all depends on how bad you want that Grimoire thing and how much you know about it." Banneker got slowly down off his horse. Brittle bones snapped under his feet. He bent over to wipe human dust from his pants cuff

and pulled a derringer from his boot.

"Don't let this upset you." He held the weapon as if he were offering a cheap cigar. "A fella told me once that if a man pulls a gun on you and doesn't shoot right away, it's because he doesn't really want to kill you."

"Is that a fact?" Hinchley matched Banneker's easy tone effortlessly.

"Nossir, it ain't. Because I purely want to kill you. I just don't think I could do the three of you." He glanced at squat, hairy, Slasher Jim Trask, caught the glint of deadly malice in his eyes, and looked away, toward *Dona* Maria. again.

Her eyes were worse.

"So let's talk business."

"We're listening. But be brief. *La Dona* Maria Sophia is losing her patience. And you don't want to see that happen. Nor do I."

"All right. You probably think I'm carrying that book with me. I may be. But maybe not. And if you kill me and it's not in here—" He patted the canvas bag strapped to his saddle. "Who you gonna ask where it is?"

Hinchley turned to Maria Sophia. "We have a clever man here, eh, *Dona* Maria?'

"I'm smart enough to know you can't look in this bag unless you kill me first." He held the derringer a little tighter.

"Mister Banneker, it's painfully obvious to me you have the Grimoire in that cottonball sack," Hinchley sighed.

"Ninety percent chance you're right. You want to take it?"

He sighed again. "What's your offer?"

"My offer is I tell you where the book is and what I know about it, and you don't kill me. None of you. Nor mortally wound me, leave me tied up in the hot sun with wet leather cord, hanging from a tree, staked to an ant-hill, paralyzed from neck-breaking, dismembered, blinded, tongue cut out..."

"He wastes our time." *Dona* Maria Sophia Vales got gracefully down from the wagon, picked up the gun from the dead hand of Pepe Avocado, who had died loving her, and leveled it at Banneker.

Big Bob Banneker spun toward her, pointing the derringer. She was more than thirty feet away, an unlikely target for the little gun, but his options were limited.

"Maria!" Hinchley's composure suddenly crumbled. "Don't kill him!"

Banneker heard the panic in his voice, realized his bargaining position was stronger than he thought.

But not strong enough.

Dona Maria fired. Her shot missed Banneker by inches.

"I said don't kill him, Maria!"

She fired again. For a fraction of a second, Banneker wondered why Hinchley sounded so panicked, then focused on the immediate concern of getting shot at.

Slasher Jim Trask moved toward her. Maria sent a round his way to no effect.

Big Bob crouched down next to a broken crate to make himself a smaller target. The result was barely noticeable. He fired at *Dona* Maria and missed.

"Maria!" Hinchley screamed again, louder and desperate. "DON'T!

Dona Maria took another shot at Banneker. A good one. Big Bob screamed in pain as the bullet struck just below the knee. He dropped the derringer and doubled up, more hurt than he'd ever known before. Somewhere behind him, he heard Trask and Hinchley moving about... He blinked tears from his eyes and looked around for *Dona* Maria

She was looking at him.

No, above him.

And behind him.

And Screaming!

Banneker squeezed his eyes closed, expecting a shot from her pistol.

It never came.

Dona Maria Sophia shuddered under the impact of the heavy blade piercing her body. Reeled backwards. Hit the hard ground.

And died in the arms of the man who loved her.

Banneker opened his eyes. For a brief instant, he saw something. Or rather, his eyes kept sending him images his mind could not accept. As he quickly lost consciousness, he realized he must be seeing things...

Then he knew nothing.

CHAPTER 33

"Something up ahead," Harvey said.

I squinted up the road and all I got for my trouble was a shapeless smudge piled up on one side. Looked no bigger than a pebble from here.

"I swear, Harve', there's times I think you can see around corners. I can't hardly even see that thing, much less say what it is."

"Just as well." He looked thoughtful. "We'll get to it soon enough."

I got a feeling there was something up there I wasn't going to like, and Harvey knew it was there and didn't want to tell me about it. But I likewise knew by now that if Harvey didn't want to say something, it just wasn't going to get said at all. So I moved the talk back around to where it had been:

"Something else about that Grimswaller book I can't figure. What I heard was, there's spells in it, words you can say that will summon up the Devil."

"They say that." Harvey allowed. "It's a misunderstanding."

"You never did seem to me like the kind of puppy that jumps up and comes running when he's called."

"But I am, you know." He stretched in the saddle. "I told you once before; I said, 'Streak my boy,' I said, 'My arms are always open for the sinner who will come unto me."

I remembered now. "Yeah, you and Jesus."

"That's just about all we have in common."

"So I hear. Good and evil."

"I like to think it's more a matter of style. I sail easy and go with the breeze, where Christ runs a tight ship but..."

"How's that again?"

"Scriptures say you got to believe in Christ to get into heaven. And some folks hold that you got to prove it by getting dunked in the river, or putting ash on your head, calling out His name..."

"Where you leading all this, Harvey?"

"I'm just saying a man has to jump through some hoops to get into Heaven. Them folks that beat the drum for Jesus, they all say He's the forgiving sort, but some of 'em's mighty picky about which knee to get down on, and how much you chip into the pot." He paused for a beat or maybe two.

Then, "No such nonsense about Hell. Anybody can get in, and welcome to 'em. You don't even have to mention my name." We were getting close to whatever-it-was in the road by now. "Speaking of which, I'm going to bow out of things for a bit. I'll catch up to you at the Doctor's in Retrospect."

"Doctor's? I don't plan to—"

But he'd gone.

And just about then, I rode up on the thing in the road. And I seen as how the Devil'd been right not to tell me what it was.

The Fargo wagon. Same one we used as a scaffold for Pug Klavinsky. The wagon full of crates of heathen bones that Hinchley and Trask stole from us.

But all the crates we'd had stacked up and strapped down, every last blasted one of them was busted open and the bones inside scattered all over everywhere.

And just to this side of it, part-hidden in the evening shadows, there was a body. A big one.

"Big Bob!" I was already out of the saddle and kicking my way over smashed boxes and broken bones to get to it.

And about the time I got there, Big Bob raised one hand and said, "Don't hurry. I'm not going anywhere real soon."

Brought me to a sudden stop, it did. I took a good look down at him and saw he'd tore off his shirt and wrapped it around his knee.

It was soppy wet with blood.

"Couldn't get it tight enough to stop the bleeding," he said. "Like to died."

"I'm not sure you didn't." I peeled off my neckerchief and fixed it around his leg for a proper blood-stopper. "How's that feel?"

"Hurts like a sunuvabitch."

"I bet it does."

"You reckon you could get me into that wagon and on to Retrospect?"

"I can."

"Fine by me."

"Guess I'm working for you again."

"As long as you don't ever remind me I let you go."

"Good enough."

CHAPTER 34

"They must've just left me there to ponder my sins," Big Bob said, "I think maybe they couldn't come up with anything worse than bleeding to death from a shot knee. All I know is I was plumb out of my head when they killed the woman. Watch out for that tree root up ahead."

Big Bob never asked about Harvey or nothing. Didn't seem to remember him at all. Like a hole opened up in his mind and the Devil slipped down it.

"I can't offhand think of anything worse myself. This bunch is like hot corn on a skillet, popping ever which of a way..." I managed to steer the horses around a root grown halfway across the trail.

"You never handled a six-horse team before, didja, Streak?"

"Never did, and I'll tell the world it ain't easy."

"There's just nothing easy about this trip, but I think I've about got that Devil-book figured out." Big Bob moved himself around so as not to get jostled so much, but it didn't work. "I've puzzled on it, and got around to where I think the whole thing about stealing the Grand Grimoire, all that's just a ploy so they can sell that thing, or copies of it, to shady collectors for a better price."

"You reckon? Seems to me like way too much work and outlay for that."

"You weren't there to see it when they killed *Dona* Maria."

"You're right about that, anyhow."

"Killed her just on the off-chance they might lose the Devil Book if anything happened to me. Well, I can say for certain those two men, they've got themselfs in a lather over that book, and I can't think of any other reason than money."

"They surely wanted to make certain I wasn't there to stop 'em."

"What Hinchley called Misdirection: Get a man to look one way, then be where he ain't looking for—" The wagon hit a prairie dog hole and Big Bob stopped talking real sudden.

He was laying cross-ways in the back of the bone wagon, steadying himself up against a piece of one of them broken crates—the ones that had held sacred remains of men, Chinese men, I mean, before Hinchley and Trask busted up the whole lot of them. The fresh bodies—the Vales woman and Pepe Avocado—laid cross-ways next to him, and sometimes he braced himself with his elbow pushing on one or the other of 'em. Didn't seem to bother him none.

"Did you get a chance to look close at all those busted crates?"

"Too busy lookin' after you, Boss."

"Me neither. But I'm looking close at this one here."

"And?"

"It wasn't pried open. Looks more like it got picked up and smashed on a rock or just pulled apart maybe. Likeways with the zinc boxes that were inside the crates, now I come to study on it. They look like somebody just tore 'em open or maybe picked 'em up and—Owwww!!"

"Sorry, Big Bob."

"Ahhh, you're not doing too bad, Streak. No worse than a one-armed blind man, anyhow."

"Don't go spoiling me with sweet talk."

"I won't. What I want now is for you to tell me who or what scattered those heathen bones all over the countryside and how they did it."

"I'm not for askin'. Still can't make much sense of what you said happened to Pepe." I yanked reins some more again, but it seemed like those Fargo horses got themselves headed into Retrospect more from their own memory than my driving. "You telling me he killed himself just because that Vales woman told him to?"

"I can't say for certain, but that's purely how it looked to me. Like she'd got some power over him. Yeah, and she never tried it on me," he moaned soft-like. "I just about wish she had!"

"I guess he sure enough loved that woman."

"I don't think so, Streak. I don't think it at all."

"Didn't you see how he looked at her?"

"I saw it all right." He looked down at the two dead bodies riding in the back with him. "And I saw how she looked back at him, right through him and clear to next Christmas. It wasn't love. Not an ounce of love in two tons of how they felt for each other."

I urged the wagon up a small grade, and Big Bob pounded the floor of that wagon bed with the pain of shifting around. Then he went on,

"He worshipped her. That little mouse of a man worshipped that big, beautiful lady. And Worship ain't the same as Love. I've seen 'em both, seen 'em close-up, and they just ain't the sa—UNGH!"

We topped the rise, and the load in back shifted again, which got me another moan from Big Bob. He cussed me, cussed the road, cussed the horses, cussed the world in general, and kept right on cussing till we came up near to a church and he quieted down some so as not to let God hear him carrying on.

It wasn't actually a church, I guess. It had been once, maybe, but right now it was an old abandoned Spanish mission, halfway fallen down. The road ran right up by it, close enough to see through the holes in the walls into the dark, peaceful insides and feel the cool air drift out on the breeze.

And right beyond that, the town of Retrospect.

CHAPTER 35

I got to say it was some bustling place, too. There was still enough light for me to see fully three blocks long and three blocks deep, with a two-story brick courthouse, a fancy theatre, swank-looking hotel, saloons, and I don't know what-all, but after spending a week in Gunder's Station it surely made a sight.

"Drop me at the Fargo Office so's I can file a report." Big Bob kind of groaned when he said it, and I near laughed out loud.

"I hate to disobey an order, me being new-hired, and you the boss and all," I said, "But I'm taking you directly to the first doctor we come to, and then call the local law in to take 'em a look at these here dead folks riding with you."

"Fine, let's just swing by the Fargo Office first, it's on the way and…"

I didn't hear the rest, being too busy steering the rig to a clean-looking place I'd just spotted on the left, under a sign "D. M. RETTER, MD." Big Bob hollered and cursed me for a yaller dog, but then he got serious-like. "Streak, we need to pull our heads together whilst mine's still working right—before some sawbones comes out and cuts my leg off at the neck."

"Okay, just let me run inside and—"

"You stay where you are. We can wait till whosomever's in there sees the crowd we're getting up here and—ungh!"

He was right on one subject; we were drawing a sizeable assembly of the idle curious type, and one of them jostled the wagon. Bob let out a quiet scream and told him to do something that didn't sound at all decent.

"Either that," he finished up with, "Or get inside and hunt up the Doctor." He turned back to me. "The thing is this: You got no way of knowing it..."

Just about then, this Doc Retter—the one it talked about on the sign hung out there—this Doc Retter come out and barked at the folks around to get up off their butts and carry Bob inside—careful of that leg. Took some doing, but they got him in and laid him down on a table, and I got me a look at the good doctor.

He measured on the short side, a small man with a big voice and an even bigger hogleg hung from his belt. I wondered what kind of practice he had, to go around equipped like that, and I guess he noticed me noticing.

"Don't usually go heeled." He bent over to look close at Big Bob's knee. "I lost one last month. Lost a patient, I mean. Got the bullet out of his lung but couldn't clear stop the bleeding. Infection set in, took him about a week to die, and by then he'd talked himself and his gun buddies into thinking it was my fault. I had to persuade one or two of them out of the notion. Marshal's no help here. Had to do it my own self..."

"All that's powerful fascinating," Big Bob said, "But I got to confer with my associate here., Wonder if you could back up and go off in the distance a while."

But that Retter, he paid no heed. Just bent over close, looked at Big Bob's knee, and came out with a medical opinion.

"Horse knuckles! Bullet made a hairline crack on the kneecap and bounced clear. Nothing I can do but bind it up and tell you to stay off it."

"How's if you clean it up some first while you're about it?"

"If you're going to be fussy about it, sure."

"Streak, where'd you find this meat-cutter?"

"Now listen, if you're going to be insulting—"

"Easy up, Doc." I raised a hand to make peace. "Big Bob here's hurting and he just naturally ain't at his best. Been hurting quite a while, too, and I can say for truth that even when he ain't hurt, he's got a hard-traveling way on him."

"And that's a taller story than Paul Bunyan." Big Bob sat up. He regretted it, too. Tried not to let it show, but I could tell from the way he screamed that it hurt a little.

"See how I mean, Doc?" I put a hand on Big Bob's shoulder and pushed him back down. "Reckon he's near-delirious and not responsible. But he's a good man—underneath—and I'd take it as a personal favor if you'd not mind his talk and do what you can for him."

"Well, put it that way…" He wadded up a cloth and handed it to me. "Give him that to bite out his screams on while I work."

Big Bob took hold of that cloth and tried to slap Retter's face with it, but the Doc was a fast-moving man. "I said we was to talk." He grabbed my arm. "So you best listen, else I'll bite out them screams on your gun hand. On account of my head's clearing up and I keep thinking back on how that Donna Maria died and it-and it… Those two is bad trouble. Hinchley and Trask. You're going after 'em, ain't you?"

"Figgered I would."

"Yeah, and I figgered as much. But they-they-they're more trouble than… You don't try 'em alone, 'cause…"

Bob quit talking on account of he passed out sound asleep. I turned back to Doc Retter.

"What was you telling me on this Marshal man?"

"Marshal Cobb MacLewin. A good man when he's sober. Or so they tell me."

"You never seen him sober?"

"Never seen him do anything. Good or otherwise. Of any kind. What you want him for anyway?"

"Thought he might like to do something about Big Bob here getting knee-shot and robbed. The men that did it are likely here in town. And those two dead ones I brought in—"

"Not unless any of this happened here in Retrospect."

"Wasn't more than a half-hour distant"

"That's all MacLewin needs to put it out of his mind and send you on a fool's errand to the County Sheriff, two day's ride from here."

"Don't he care about who gets robbed and killed around these parts?"

"Not so's you'd notice. When the City Fathers hired him to keep the noise down, they wrote the contract so's he'd be handy when they needed him, not running around the countryside chasing varmints. His jurisdiction ends at the city limits, and—this is important to him—so does his paycheck."

"What you mean is unless somebody busts things up here in Retrospect..." I thought of something. "Big Bob there told me once how it's a crime to have something on you that was stolen."

He chewed on that one for a time, then,

"I suppose that's a chance."

"Then I'll take it."

CHAPTER 36

"Marshal's office is just over the next block." Harvey was waiting for me outside the Doctor's place. "Got the makings on you?"

I'd got used to this coming-and-going business of his by now, and it didn't surprise me none. I handed him the tobacco pouch and cigarette papers, and we headed down the next block whilst he rolled him a smoke.

"Don't they let you take pouch and papers down to Hell?"

"There's no *They* about it." He took a deep draw and blew a smoke ring. "I make the rules down there. I tried keeping the makings around, but folks kept stealing it, and running behind the barn to sneak a smoke." He took another thoughtful draw. "The place is full of thieves."

"I'm not surprised."

"Sometimes I think I should raise the rents and see if I get a classier clientele."

"Let me know how that works out for you."

"But I guess a man in my line of work ought to get used to low company." We'd reached the Marshal's office by now, and Harvey pushed the door part-open. "Shall we try our chances with the Marshal?"

CHAPTER 37

"**N**ot a chance," Marshal MacLewin talked quiet, no louder than what a barber makes brushing you off, but he talked like he meant it, and had a mind that wasn't about changing. "Not a Chinaman's chance."

"Wells Fargo's offering a reward," Harvey said.

The lawman eyed him close, like he was trying to place a familiar face. "I'll get my hat."

From what Doc Retter said, I was expecting Marshal MacLewin to be a gutless wonder butt-branded by the easy chair, but this here peace officer looked more like Bill Hickock or Deadeye Davis, with maybe a touch of the Earp Brothers in the mix. He carried a pair of twin Colt 45s—plain, but shiny as sunlight off a dewleaf—reversed on his belt for a cross draw, and I could see the handle of a Bowie Knife sticking up from a fancy-beaded Apache sheath on his belt.

But it wasn't the hardware that made him look tough; it was his eyes. They were pale blue, bloodshot, and I'm not sure if this is the right word, but they were inert. Not dead, but more like they never had lived. No more feeling in them than a river rock has for the cold water flowing over it.

That hat he mentioned was a low-crown Stetson, black with a wide brim. He wore his fair hair long, like Custer did before Crazy Horse barbered him up, and likewise his moustaches swept from his nose all the ways down to his chin, then back up clear to his cheek bones.

I bet the ladies fair swooned on him.

"Now what's this about a ree-ward?" He pulled a bottle and two shot glasses from a desk drawer and toted them over. Harvey threw him a big wide smile.

"A thousand in Gold for the arrest and conviction of parties who etc. etc."

"A thousand in Gold?" MacLewin filled a shot glass for Harvey, then one for himself, right to the brim. "Fargo's getting generous lately!"

"Yes, aren't they?" Harvey sipped at his drink. "Well, it's only talk, after all."

"How's that?"

"Money, Marshal. I'm talking of money."

"Then here's to crime." MacLewin touched his glass to Harvey's, then raised it to me like he was proposing a toast. "When you're older, Kid."

I got to say it rubbed me wrong. Rubbed me hard, it did, and I was readying me to say a thing or two about it when Harvey spoke up.

"Careful how you talk to this one, Marshal. This here's Streak Wilson."

"The Fargo shotgun guard?" He downed his drink and poured another.

"I reckon so," I said.

"I've heard about you."

I couldn't tell from his voice if that was a good thing for me or not, so I just gave out with "Have you?" which seemed safest to say.

"Mostly lies, I reckon." He looked me up and down. Did a thorough job of it, but made it look like just a casual glance. "There's places where you're not exactly popular, but the brass hats in their warm little offices think you do your job okay."

"And what do you think?"

"I haven't formed an opinion on the subject. Had you figured for an older man."

"I hope to become one."

"Take your time, then. And don't hope too hard on it if you plan on staying in this line of work." He downed the second drink without even thinking about it, like it was habit in him or something. "You say it's Headless Hinchley and Slasher Jim Trask,?"

"You know 'em?"

"Not personal, but there's something…" He scanned a bulletin board covered with pictures and the word WANTED all over it. Then he went to his desk, poured himself another drink, and opened a deep drawer like I never saw before.

This drawer had a sign on the front that said FILE, but it wasn't built to hold tools. Deep and exactly wide as a sheet of paper, full of wanted notices, letters and such-like, set on their edges, packed tight to hold in place. Every so often there was a bookmark sticking up with a capital letter on it. First he went to the letter H, then to T and he pulled a paper out from each.

"Just like I thought," he grinned. "These two is dead."

Well that stirred up some controversy, it did.

"Marshal, I'm not calling you a liar, but me and the man I work for spent most of today trying to keep these two dead men from killing us. And I brought in two shot bodies they left as calling cards."

"And I'm not calling you a liar either, kid. It's just as how these here death notices say you must have got yourself mistaken maybe. Take a looky-see." MacLewin passed a creased-up paper my way, and I was looking at a picture of Slasher Jim Trask and a note on the back said he got a bullet in him from the Texas Rangers.

"And this one some while back, I forget when." There wasn't any date on the paper, just a picture of Hinchley, and writing on the back about him being executed by a court martial back in the war.

Harvey looked over the notices with me and just smiled. "If those two men are dead, they've got a right funny way of showing it, Marshal."

I couldn't plumb it. Two men I'd seen walking, talking, riding and fighting every bit of just today. Then I saw something else, a note below the notes, same note on each one, and it said, "Body not Recovered."

I handed the bulletin back. "How can you hang a man and lose his body?"

"It don't say, so I don't know," MacLewin tucked the bulletins into his coat pocket. "But if we find these jaspers, maybe they'll tell us what they did with their own dead bodies."

And I guess we would of gone out right then gunning for Hinchley and Trask, or their ghosts maybe—if it weren't for the man from China.

CHAPTER 38

The man from China came in the door just when we were fixing up to go out of it, and if I told all about him, I'd have to write a whole book on the subject.

For one thing, he didn't talk English but he thought he did. He'd learned the words, only he said them all wrong. Bad wrong. Wrong enough that if he'd asked "Pass the potatoes," we'd of thought he told us to burn down the outhouse.

Slowed things up considerable.

This jackeroo, I think his name was Dashou, but it was hard telling, the way he talked. He wore a plain black coat, kind of like the preachers do, except the sleeves were wide, for a reason I found out later. He wasn't tall, and he wasn't much for muscle, but he had a way of moving himself around like a man who could look out for himself. Or maybe just a man to look out for.

And he had a trick of putting himself just enough in the way that we had to stay and listen, or else knock him down to get past him, which none of us felt like trying. So there was nothing for it but to work ourselves at figuring out what he was trying to say.

Turned out his business was with the remains scattered out by the road into town, what Big Bob Banneker called them Heathen Bones that weren't ever going to get back to the graves of their ancestors now. No, they weren't, not ever, Dashou said; somebody'd wrecked that beyond repair, and he wanted to have a little visit with 'em and spoil their day over it.

At about which time the Marshal got a look on his face that said plain as dirt that he didn't give a stink in the wind over what Dashou wanted, nor a pee in the ocean about Dashou himself, and as for his ancestors...

And like I said, the man from China didn't speak good English, but he could read that look on the lawman's face as good as I could, and he gave him a look right back that a blind man could read: BAD ROAD YONDER. TURN BACK. Marshal MacLewin saw that look all right, and he didn't like it much.

But then Harvey says, quiet-like, "If you want to kill him, go ahead. No law against killing a Chinee, but it's going to waste a lot of time, and by now--" He flipped his ace on the table. "--word's got out about that reward."

The Devil's a good judge of character. MacLewin unwound his mayhem spring, and Dashou stopped glaring like Yellow Murder. Harvey looked pleased with himself and I--

"You reckon you can find them?" I asked MacLewin. It was full dark now, but it was Saturday night, and the streets were lit up like a cow town: boardwalks crowded with folks out for a good time, saloons elbowed up, and, I guess I've seen some pretty important places since I started riding for Wells Fargo, even been to Dodge City and Abilene, but this here town of Retrospect was as full of hustle-and-shove as any of them.

"Well now," Marshal MacLewin stroked his chin kind of thoughtful-like. "I'd suppose we got even odds of it. I used to know a man that used to brag on how he run Slasher Jim Trask out of Placerville, long ago back. And nobody called Headless Hinchley is gonna be very hard to recognize." He left off scratching his chin. "And I think I know where to pick up the trail…"

He led us over to the next block, where I could see the Opera House, all lighted and bannered, and folks outside reading the posters, and when we got up closer, I could read the sign.

CHAPTER 39

Themthere it was, in letters a foot high:

HINCHLEY & TRASK!
PRESENT
} FOR ONE NIGHT ONLY{
Direct from the Halls of Incunabula
SECRETS OF THE NEW AGE!
REVELATIONS!!
DEATH OF SATAN!!!!

THE OLD GODS RETURN!!!!!!

MYSTERY-MURDER of the MISSING MANUSCRIPT
FATE traps the GUILTY!
Lecture & Demonstration
by
H.H. Hinchley
&
S. James Trask, esq.

And somebody had pasted a banner across all that, bright yellow with big blue printing:

FINAL PERFORMANCE!

"Well, I'll be cheese!" MacLewin made out like he was surprised. "Looks like we stumbled over a clue or something! What do you make of it, boys?"

I was already thinking what to do next and how to do it. "You know the layout in there, Marshal?"

He nodded. "I was aiming to get in and settle those two before the crowd got here—" He shot a glance over at Dashou. "Only we got delayed some, didn't we?"

There was maybe a flicker in Dashou's eyes, but I couldn't be sure, because the rest of him was purely inscrutable, which is a fancy word I learned for Poker-Face.

"Yeah, and it took a while and then some to sign you up, Marshal. Now I'm wondering how to get backstage and lay hands on a couple of mad dogs. You know the way well enough to lead?"

"I do for a fact. So I'll do you a favor and not take you there. Come down to it, Mister Wilson, I won't even tell you the way, 'cause I estimate you're just too young to get torn apart by an angry mob."

He nodded over at the crowd going in. Well-dressed and genteel in manner, mostly. And those that weren't well-dressed were dressed as well as they could. Even from here, I could nose out barber lotion, store-bought baths, and Sunday clothes over the smell of cowboy sweat and trail dirt.

"Folks here get awful hungry for entertainment," MacLewin went on, "Some of them paid a dollar just to stand in the back and see this. Hell, I once seen a man force his way in at gunpoint just to watch HAMLET."

I studied the crowd a little closer and begun to catch his drift.

"Halfway through the show, this drama desperado, he shot the actor playing the King. Busted up the whole shebang. Somebody got his gun away from him, and those prim and proper Thee-ater Go-ers... well, I've seen lynchings nicer than what they done to him."

"I take the feeling you don't want to do much about these two till after the show."

"And I can see you're learning fast."

"You got any notion what to do next?"

"Just one: watch the show." MacLewin turned, looked around. "They hold seats for the local gentry, and I can badge my way into some. You plan to tote that long gun in with you?"

"Plan to, yes."

"I better get me a box seat then." He nodded in the general direction of Dashou. "You find it needful to take him along?"

I checked out Dashou and read it on his face that he'd heard every word of that and didn't like it much.

"I ain't gonna try and talk him out of it."

"Definite for box then. How about your pal Harvey?" He looked around again. "What become of him?"

"Him and fightin' don't mix up much."

"Ducked out, did he?

"He don't involve himself without he gets paid for it."

"A hired gun can be useful. "

"You don't want to pay what he charges. Leastways, I think you don't." I considered on it. "Come to that, mostly folks don't notice him slipping off like he does."

"I'm part dog." MacLewin smiled. "I can always tell a bad'un, and don't ever take my eyes off 'em."

Dashou just nodded.

CHAPTER 40

"**B**est seats in the house?" The Devil asked.

I'd turned down the Marshal's offer of box seats. Me and Harvey had our butts perched on a wooden rail that ran along a thing they call the Catwalk, way up high in the dark among the rafters, maybe fifty feet or more above the stage. I found a hook to hang my Spencer rifle on—plenty of heavy hooks up there, I guess for hanging scenery and curtains and the like. There were two stagehands up there too, right close to us, moving around like they were used to looking down from on high, way up here, hauling stuff around, readying up a candle torch and something that looked like a block of— I moved up a little closer to them.

"Is that there quicklime?"

"Sure is." The one closest to me nodded, his white hair reflecting what light there was up there. "And I don't aim to get none on me answering stupid questions. Burns like acid." He set it on some kind of platform and busied himself with it.

"I don't even see why we got to fool around with it." His partner's raspy voice echoed softly on the wooden ceiling. "Ain't like we're gonna use it much here."

"Quiet, Clyde!" White-hair jerked a thumb in my direction so's his partner could see and shut up. "He wants it to look good, and as long as he's paying…"

The one named Clyde set to work, and I saw now that the platform with the block of quicklime on it had hinges on the sides, and as he flipped them up and snapped them together, they made a box with a big round hole in the front and a smaller one in back. I thought it looked pretty interesting, but I was curiouser about whatever it was they didn't want to say in front of me.

"Didja see that fancy poster out front?" he went on, "Paid me in promises. Said the real payoff's gonna be the Mission Show—"

Silver-hair cut him off with a short move of his hands and a nod in my direction, then come over on the catwalk right quick and gave me a sharp-edge look. "You sure the Marshal sent you up here, Kid?"

"You can go down and ask him, if it bothers you, Old Timer." It shouldn't have peeved me like it did, him calling me Kid. But it did, and I was too tired to hold it in. "If you think those legs'll carry you."

"I got legs." He looked real serious now. "Question is: Do you got wings, Kid?"

I studied his face. Hadn't caught sight of it before, but I could see now there was a streak of Mean real evident. Up there in the shadows, I'd took him for an old man, but now I saw that silver hair and pale skin were on account of he was albino. Maybe touchy over getting teased for it.

Sensitive type that he was, he'd took two steps closer to me, and only needed maybe one or two more to get within pushing-off-the-catwalk-range. I felt my mind start working like it always does lately: Calculating how much danger he was to me, how much time I had to kill him before he closed in, and how much I hated to kill a man over a few spilled words.

I took a step back. Then another. And so on till I found a solid upright beam next to me and put an arm around it. Whitie quit coming my way, just sneered at me, made sure I saw it, then went back to work.

"Sure is hard to make friends in high places." Harvey looked down the fifty feet or so to the stage and sighed him a good one.

"Up here looks to me like the best place to watch the exits back and front," I said. "Marshal's watching from that little balcony." I pointed to him, relaxing, feet-up, in a cup-shaped nest on the wall. "And that Dashou feller, he's covering the other side."

"Keeps 'em apart, anyhow." Harvey nodded.

"Funny thing: That Marshal sees you come and go. Most folks don't notice, but he does. Have you two done business?"

"I'm going to answer that with a question, Streak," Harvey said, "If you'd made a deal with me, would you want me telling every Tom and Chester what was the price you put on your immortal soul?"

"Sorry I asked. Didn't think it through."

"Well, don't stay up nights fretting over it. You probably know the answer already."

I got kind of a shiver over that.

"I just can't figure out about that book and whatever good it's likely to do these jaspers?"

I knew that was the sad truth of it, but there was something else troubling my mind. That word Banneker had said to me.

Misdirection.

Only I never had time to say it because over at the lights, Whitey and Clyde set a fire inside that box, the one with holes and a block of quicklime in it, and next thing, the brightest light you ever did see come out and lit up a circle right in the middle of the stage. A big drum from down in a pit in front started pounding a fanfare. I stared down at where the light made a circle on the stage…

And then, out of the corner of my eyes, I caught a quick flash of something behind the stage. Just a blink of motion, *a different shade of darkness…*

The drum got louder.

… like a door opening and closing…

The drum beat got faster.

… quick and quiet! I looked back at the limelight on the stage

But nothing happened.

After a while, the drum stopped beating.

The men on the catwalk got out a heavy coal shovel, picked up the block of quicklime, and put it in a heavy metal box. They didn't get close to that burning lump for more'n a few seconds, but when they closed the lid on the box, they were sweating all over.

Lights came up in the hall, and folks commenced to get restless, then they got loud, and they was just on the edge of getting rowdy when Marshal MacLewin touched off his shotgun. Inside that hall, the noise like to blew out my eardrums, and it sure put the fear of God in the crowd down below.

"You ladies and gents just remember you're ladies and gents." He didn't holler, exactly, but his voice filled the place up anyhow. "Don't you be crying and carrying on like common folk. Get yourselves lined up, write your names on a list someplace and we'll see about getting your money back."

"I want my money back NOW!" Whoever yelled it sounded drunk, but a lot of folks seemed to like what he said.

Didn't flap the Marshal much, though. "Anyone who wants their money back right now, just come up here, and I'll see you get what you're asking for." That dampened things down right quick.

But I wasn't there to see it.

CHAPTER 41

Things were just starting to quiet down in that theater when Harvey and me got out a side door and through the crowd that was spilling out—mostly into a close-by saloon. We didn't see Marshal MacLewin nor Dashou, and that was all right for me, 'cause I didn't want either one of them slowing us down.

We were headed to a livery stable, took maybe fifteen minutes to get there, and just a half-tick beyond the time we came in, we were studying hoof-prints from the stalls where two men had stabled their mounts—prior to riding out of here...

"Let me see that mud they churned up, Harvey." I felt it squeeze between my fingers. "It's fresh-broke and lots of it. I'd say they pulled out of here in a hurry just about the same time as the theatre crowd got restless in their seats."

I studied the tracks, and they looked like mustangs to me. Small-built, tough little horses, tamed by Apaches and bred by nature to cover more ground in rough country than many a better horse. Just what a man wants under him when he's in a mood to travel far and farther.

"You gents looking for something hereabouts, are you?"

It was the stableman. Broad-chested, long of arm from pitching hay, and gentle-mannered, if you'd overlook the scythe he carried on his shoulder when he come up behind us. And he wasn't alone, neither. A lot of the theater-going public had got the same idea I had, and they were crowded up behind him.

"You know who just got out of here on the horses from these stalls?"

Somebody behind him yelled, "Was it them?"

The stable man looked from me back to the crowd like he didn't know who to answer. Then he came out with, "Was it who?" and two or three fancy dudes in the mob began to talking loud and fast at him all to the same time, and he wasn't paying any mind to me at all, just trying to answer questions that came too sudden for him to get right.

I studied the tracks. One of the mustangs must have had an off-leg; I could see that from the length between the tracks. And a shoe on the other one was bent-up just a tad. They'd be easy to follow. I pushed my way through all the hollering folks the stable man was trying to handle.

"...A tall man, skinny, well-dressed, and the other one was short, kind of hairy..."

Outside the door, I could read the tracks easy in the moonlight. Headed north, towards open country. Closest town would be two days' ride...

"That's them!" Somebody yelled, "They can't have got far! Let's get 'em!"

And then there was a general rush to saddle anything in the barn with four legs, and next thing I knew, must have been a dozen men riding out that door after those tracks.

In the quiet afterwards, I turned back to Harvey.

"Misdirection," I said.

CHAPTER 42

I never in my life saw a Moon near as bright as that night, not before nor since, rising up over the crumbling old Spanish mission on the outskirts of town, and shining down on what was left of the mission bell tower, and the tile roof, shining like the limelight in the Opera House.

Harvey and I moved up on it—I mean the mission, not the Moon—from one patch of shadow to the next, and once we made it in close, I spotted footprints in the sandy ground leading to a side door near the front.

A plentiful lot of them, all going in...

"You said something about these Devil-Worshippers liked to meet in old churches," I said it soft-voice. There wasn't any need to whisper, but I didn't want to announce us either.

"It's a fact."

"And I noticed on the way into town, this place didn't spook me any."

That's a funny thing with me. Ever since I made Harvey's acquaintance, I been leery of churches—most of 'em anyhow. It's hard to describe how I feel around a church, it's like feeling a blackfly or a hornet buzzing touch-and-go at the back of my neck. Can't make myself go in one, and don't want to try anymore.

But I didn't feel any of that here.

From inside there come a noise like people praying out loud, but I still didn't get uncomfortable like in a church, so I knew it wasn't that. I eased in, careful not to frame myself in the doorway, and looked around as best I could, waiting for my eyes to adjust to the darker dark in there.

Something was wrong.

There should have been somebody watching the door, if what I thought was going on inside was...

"We took care of them already."

It was Marshal MacLewin, whispering from somewhere close in the dark. I managed not to jump out of my skin—not clear out, anyhow—and looked around. My eyes got a little more used to the dark, and things started to take on form and look real.

We were in a fair-sized room, what they call the vestibule, just off the main room—I read in a book that they call that big room the nave sometimes, but back in Arkansas we just called it the Meetin' Room. Anyhow, we were right outside it, like the lobby in a theater. Big double-doors muffled the prayer-noise from inside, but not much. There was something dark and funny-shaped behind the Marshal; I stared at it, and pretty quick I seen it was Dashou, half-crouched, near invisible in his black clothes. I found my voice again.

"How'd you two get here?" There wasn't much need to whisper, what with the prayer-voices coming louder and louder from the next room, but I whispered anyway.

"I got ways." MacLewin looked past me at Harvey. "You're coming in, too?"

"That's right," Harvey said it like there was some other meaning in the words. "Just for the cleaning-up."

"Is it right now?" MacLewin asked.

"Pretty soon," Harvey said.

Behind the Marshal, Dashou half-nodded, like he understood there was something going on here beyond the words. I wished he'd explain it to me.

"Let's take us a look, before we bust up the dance." MacLewin eased open one of the double doors, pulled it noiselessly wide open so's all of us could see inside and hear the praying better.

No, it wasn't praying.

They were chanting in there.

Repeating something in words I couldn't make out.

"Satanas eos sanos facite."

"Satanas facite eis ut vivant iterum."

And every time they said it, they got louder.

"Satanas eos sanos facite!"

"Satanas facite eis ut vivant iterum!"

And faster.

"Satanas eos sanos facite! Satanas facite eis ut vivant iterum!"

"Satanas eos sanos facite! Satanas facite eis ut vivant iterum! Satanas eos sanos facite! Satanas facite eis ut vivant iterum! "Satanas eos sanos facite! Satanas facite eis ut vivant iterum!"

"Satan make them whole again," Harvey translated it under his breath as we eased inside. "Satan make them live again."

There was maybe forty or fifty-some folks sitting on benches, staring up front at the raised place where they had the altar and all that truck, where the Padre used to give out sermons, back when this was a mission church.

They call that raised-up part the sanctuary, only now the crosses was all turned upside down, and the scripture marks on the altar scratched off with big five-point stars gouged in the wood. And up there at the front, Hinchley and Trask were leaning over a manger set up on a fancy-carved table, and that Devil-Book, the book men had killed for and got killed for, it was open on the table, with a spotlight on it.

MacLewin pointed up to something like a choir loft behind us, where the spotlight was coming from.

He didn't have to say it. No telling who was up there with that light, nor what amount of deadly they might be toting, but we wouldn't want 'em behind us when the party started.

I cradled the Spencer rifle in my arms and moved to the foot of a narrow staircase going up. Then I just stopped at the foot of the stairs, held my breath and listened.

Shut my ears to the chanting in the next room, and I listened to the old mission: The building itself. The faint *crack!* of adobe bricks cooling off in the night and settling into each other just a little closer. The distant groaning of old timbers, the rustle of mice in the walls, bats and nightbirds fluttering in at the windows up in the bell tower.

Nobody gets around without making some kind of noise, but if you listen for the natural sounds around you, there's kind of a pattern to 'em, almost like a dance. And when you get in step with it, you're moving quiet.

I started up the steps.

Slowly, resting a foot at the side of each step, close to the wall where it was strongest and less likely to creak. *One step, then two.*

My eyes were used to the inside now, and there was good enough light up ahead in the choir loft for me to see my way easy. *Another step, then one more.*

Whoever was using the spotlight, they were somewhere toward the front of the choir loft, and I was coming up the back. *Six steps up now, and six more to go.*

Likely they'd have eyes and ears forward, trained on the altar place, and if they didn't have somebody watching the stairs, I could surprise them from behind, and never fire a shot.

Eight steps up. My eyes came level with the floor, and I could see now the folks up here weren't expecting company. A light flickered somewhere up front, just a quick, small light, there-and-gone. Another light just like it came on, flickered, and died. I caught the smell of burning tobacco.

Whoever was up there had just lighted a cigarette.

Ten steps up now, and I was practically there. I stopped and considered. *That light came and went two times, so there was two men up there. Or one man who took two tries to fire up a smoke. Either way, they were taking their leisure. Wouldn't be much work to get them out of the game when—*

A baby screamed.

CHAPTER 43

Marshal MacLewin stood just outside the main room, to one side of the door, watching Streak Wilson start up the stairs. Studying the easy, practiced way he moved, cradling the rifle in a relaxed but secure grip that could be swiftly raised and aimed.

The kid knows what he's doing, the Marshal reflected. *And he didn't learn all that from Harvey.*

"He surely didn't." The Devil interrupted his thoughts. "I've been looking to recruit that boy for more'n a year now. Standoffish, though."

"Smart kid."

"You think so?"

"Right now I do." MacLewin turned his gaze away from the show inside and spoke calmly to the Devil. "Don't get me wrong, Harve'. It's been a good ride and I got no kick comin'."

"Glad you see it that way."

"It's just..." He looked back at the stairway in time to see Streak Wilson take another silent step, and his sharp eyes detected a quick flicker of light somewhere in the choir loft.

Then another. He saw Streak stiffen watchfully, then slowly relax and continue his climb. "… I wonder sometimes if I could of made it without your help. If I could of done it on my own, and how I might've turned out if—"

A baby screamed.

CHAPTER 44

Dashou gave a quick glance at the stairway as Streak Wilson started up the steps. Another quick glance at Marshal MacLewin talking to the stranger. He saw his chance.

MacLewin was vaguely aware of something in the near-darkness, like a shadow shifting in the dark, as Dahou moved through the door into the sanctuary, noiseless and insubstantial.

Dashou had known all along they were wrong. The tall, leathery-faced man and the young, fast-moving one would go about it all wrong. Their purpose was to capture or kill the two desecrators of sacred remains.

His own plans had nothing to do with capture.

Now he studied the two men standing by the altar, spotlighted and important-looking: The short one, with the body that seemed knotted together out of strong sinew and coarse hair; the slender one, whose head swung loosely when he moved, as if about to roll off his shoulders.

Dashou considered his options. It was a problem of time and motion. The short one seemed more dangerous, but the taller one might more swiftly escape on those long legs.

Did he have a choice? Even now, the hairy one had drawn his short, heavy sword and poised it above the manger.

Were the figures wavering before his eyes? Becoming more distinct somehow? *Could his eyes be getting weak?* That decided it. Dashou must kill the tall one first or risk losing him.

The short one raised his sword, preparing to bring it down in a swift, powerful arc toward the manger.

A Baby Screamed.

The sound came from the manger. Dashou turned his eye on the hairy one, and drew a sharp, gleaming hatchet from his sleeve. Sent it arcing across the room.

A shattering metallic *SMACK!* echoed from the walls, and the cutlass flew from Trask's lethal grip.

CHAPTER 45

I must have seen it and fired before I knew I was doing it, before I thought about it, maybe even before I understood it right.

From up here, you could see down into that manger on the table, past the burning limelight, between the two men in the choir loft lounging on their seats, and there was a sure-enough baby in there, laying in the manger like baby Jesus hisself. Slasher Jim Trask drew his stubby little sword...

One of the men at the spotlight took a draw on his cigarette. Trask raised the sword, like a woodchopper ready to bring the axe down...

The other man at the lights tapped ash off his smoke.

Next thing I knew, there was the sharp *Crack*! Of a rifle. I was looking down the sights of my Spencer, which was trained on that evil-looking blade down there; or where it had been, because now it was twirling across the room like a straw in a twister.

*   *   *

Down below in the sanctuary, Dashou saw his hatchet fly harmlessly past the tall one, and in a sudden moment, the world made no sense. He could not have missed. He *had not* missed! Yet his target stood there uninjured.

And angry.

The chanting stopped, noises of surprise and alarm spread through the room. Marshal MacLewin saw the movements, felt the mood shift around him in the crowd.

"Hold yer seats everybody," he announced. "There'll be some deputies along to escort everyone to the hoosegow…"

Normally, that was enough to empty a room like a shaken dustpan. But now nobody budged.

"Yea! Remain, ye who worship the Prince of Darkness." Hinchley's voice echoed across the room with the power of Night itself. "Remain! And slay the interlopers, the non-believers…"

The feel had changed in an instant. From alarm to anger. From anger to hate.

From hate to homicide.

Hands grabbed at Dashou's arms. A heavy cane grazed MacLewin's head. He staggered, reeled dizzily, saw sparks fly across the room…

*　　*　　*

I began to understand it. Two men down there, ready to kill a baby over some big ritual they believed in. A crowd of folks chanting to cheer them on, on account of they worshipped something almighty evil.

And up here, two men smoking cigarettes and putting a spotlight on the whole show, just for Money.

What I could see of the crowd down there, it was getting ugly. Real ugly. Up here, it wasn't no better. Soon as I fired, the two men on the spotlight jumped up, spun around, and stared at me, froze for a split-second when they saw the rifle...

Some time later, I wished they'd stayed froze, held still so's I could of chased them out with no killing. But right then, I was displeased something awful about anybody ready to set back, have a smoke, and watch a little baby get chopped up.

And they obliged me, both of them.

The silver-haired fella picked up a metal bar from the floor, raised it to strike, and his partner Clyde charged me head-on.

That split-second when their eyes got used to looking into the dark was all I needed to jack another round under the firing pin and send a .52 slug out of a thirty-inch barrel into the one coming at me. Stopped him in his tracks and set him back three feet into the chair he'd jumped out of.

And I ought to be ashamed to say how good that felt.

That good feeling lasted just till a heavy metal bar come swinging at my head. I ducked into it, mostly, but took a bad scrape along one ear. Started me bleeding like a gutted mule. I kept moving into the silver-haired guy, shifted the Spencer and butt-stroked him back, then back again, to the edge of the choir loft.

One more was all it took to send him head-down off the edge, but first I had to say it:

"*You* got wings?"

CHAPTER 46

I'm not proud I said that, and even less proud of how satisfied I got, seeing his head smack into a solid wood bench. I'll admit to it, though, I surely did.

Then I got a look down there, and any good feeling I ever had just crawled right up my spine.

Right below me, the whole crowd was coming at Marshal MacLewin and Dashou like Sherman run over Georgia. Up by the altar, that baby was howling louder than ever. Like to broke a strong man's heart to hear it.

And next to the manger with that kid in it, something almighty strange was going on.

Hinchley and Trask were standing close. Then closer. Then it was like neither one of them was there anymore, and yet both of them *were*. Were there, I mean, but changing...

They were merging into each other. The tall smart one and the stocky slashing one, becoming one big, hairy thing... No, it was big, but skinny-built, like that Hinchley.... No, that wasn't right, because I could see the coarse, matted hair all over it...

And the thought come to me that this thing had a body that kept on changing. Or maybe it had no body at all. Even now, as I stared down at it, I could almost see right through it and out the other side... No, wait, it was solid all right...

And this next part is hard to tell about, but that thing was powerful mad over something. Something had gone wrong someways, or some plan didn't turn out right, and the more those two changed into just one thing, the madder it was about it.

I recollected what old Heber Snow said when we were telling ghost stories, about spirits of dead people trapped here in this world because they couldn't carry their sins to Heaven and couldn't fit them into Hell. GraveWalkers, we called them.

And I remembered what Harvey said to that girl Kelly, the story about Proud Eyes and Proud Arms, merged into one, and neither could let loose of the other...

That's what the thing was there in the spotlight. A GraveWalker.

One second, it was tall like Hinchley. Next second, short and muscled up like Trask. I stared at the thing while its arms got bigger, so thick with muscle it split the seams off Hinchley's coat, and still it stood there, screaming like a caged bear, getting hairier, madder... and bone-mashing mean.

Down below, the crowd—worshippers I guess they were—seemed just tickled clear to Hell with it. Like they was fit to become beasts all on their own. They'd quit their chanting, and now they was hollering like a lynch mob gone kill-crazy, swarming at the Marshal of Retrospect and the man from China like coyotes on a carcass.

I spun the Spencer around, grabbed it by the barrel, and swung it. Swung as hard as I could.

And smashed the spotlight clear apart.

CHAPTER 47

Pieces of the box splintered and dropped on the floor, but the lump of burning quicklime inside soared off the loft and down into the crowd. Hot-burning clumps of it sprayed all over the room—so bright it hurt your eyes to see 'em—and the worshipers got a taste of Hell.

I think it changed a lot of minds.

Them as got direct hit with a burning cinder screamed and grabbed at the place, which only got their hands burned too, and they screamed louder. Started jumping, twisting, and contorting themselves across the floor like Holy Rollers at a tent-meetin'.

That was mostly, anyway. A fair amount of 'em got knocked down by the ones that got burned themselves, anyone who looked at the burning bits of quicklime too long went temporary light-blind, a few more got their clothes on fire, and then the fire caught on the benches and commenced to spreading itself around the room, which scared away even more true believers.

But not all of 'em. There was still a few fanatics dead-set on smiting the Godly, which in this case meant MacLewin and Dashou down below, plus me up here, if anybody noticed. Come to think on it, I don't believe you could call any of us exactly Godly without stretching a point or lying ouright, but the crowd down there wasn't in no mood to discuss it.

And there was still that big, hairy, shape-changing thing up by the altar, fighting inside its own body and screaming to the universe.

Things hadn't gone like they planned. The baby in the manger, the spell in that book, the chanting ritual, it was all the effort of two GraveWalkers to get themselves all the way back into living again—and away from Hell, where they belonged.

Make them whole again. Make them live again.

That's what all them devil-worshippers had been pushing, but we'd interrupted the service: Me and the Marshal of Retrospect and the man from China.

A shot cracked through the hubub down on the dance floor. MacLewin had broke free, and he was shooting his way through the crowd, up to the altar, like something from a dime novel.

Never seen anything to beat it, one man with two six-shooters barking, bodies jumping out of his way if they moved fast enough, or falling out of his way if they didn't, smoke swirling out of his gun barrels, mixing with smoke from a dozen blazing-bright little quicklime fires, and a general appearance that this man was plain unstoppable.

Then danged if he didn't march right up to the altar, past burning chunks of quicklime—never looking down at 'em, but somehow never stepping on one—right up to that table with the baby in the manger, right up to that big hairy GraveWalker that had left off screaming just to eyeball him, and he twirled his guns on his fingers and holstered 'em.

"All right," MacLewin said, calm as cold lemonade, "Just you step back, 'cause I mean to take that child out of here."

There was a blur of motion. Two blurs. The monster swung an arm out and got its massive paws around MacLewin faster than I could see it happen. And at the same time, the Marshal pulled his guns and fired point blank into its belly.

I heard the two sounds at once: The roar of twin .44s, and the crunch of bone when hairy arms squeezed, closed, and collapsed a man's lungs with one hand, then dropped a limp and lifeless body to the floor.

And turned back to the baby in the manger.

Oh hell.

There was plenty of runction going on down below. More benches had caught fire, and some folks were trying to put them out or just get out themselves. There were people burned or gun-shot, yelling their pain out to nobody listening while smoke and heat swelled around them. Wasn't easy to take a good shot, but I took two and put 'em both in the beast's ribs. It moaned in pain, turned and looked around to see where they come from, and I put another round in somewhere amidships, just to get its attention.

It worked. The GraveWalker glared up at me good and proper, and then turned like it was fixing to come up here after me, and spend some time taking me apart. Seemed to me I'd be a whole lot safer if I could get some distance between us—

But I was figuring. My shots had hurt it. Not bad enough, but I could see it was bleeding, so it must be a living thing—and if it lived, it could die, but bullets sure weren't going to kill it, and bullets were all I had to throw at it. It glared at me, and I calculated whether it was going to come at me up the stairs or just pull itself up into the loft. Looked like it could do either one pretty easy.

Then:

"*Satanas eos sanos facite! Satanas facite eis ut vivant iterum!*"
Someone started chanting.

"*Satanas eos sanos facite! Satanas facite eis ut vivant iterum!*"
Two more voices picked it up.

"*Satanas eos sanos facite! Satanas facite eis ut vivant iterum!*"
Then more.

"*Satanas eos sanos facite! Satanas facite eis ut vivant iterum!*"
Somewhere down there in the smoke and fire, and the eye-gouging light of still-burning chunks of quicklime, there were people, worshipers, folks who believed in this enough to stand up in Hell and finish the job.

The Grave-Walking monster turned back to the table, to the book.

It come to me then. The ritual had only got itself halfway done. It could still be finished and Hinchley and Trask could separate, walk as men.

Live as men.

Live…

"*Satanas eos sanos facite! Satanas facite eis ut vivant iterum!*"

There was a sudden sharp-bright flash across the room. A shiny steel hatchet skimmed through the smoke and buried itself in the floor, splintering a chunk of smoldering quicklime under the table. The GraveWalker looked up from the book just as Dashou jumped up in front of the altar, pulled his hatchet out of the floor, and lobbed a chunk of burning quicklime right at him.

The monster moved too quick for him. Went sideways fast, out of the way.

Or that's what I thought at first. Only Dashou wasn't aiming at him.

He was going for the book.

CHAPTER 48

The cinder landed square in the open pages of that devil book, smoked for a second, then commenced to burn its way clear through till there was a black hole in the middle with a little ring of brown singe at the edges and that cinder burning at the bottom of it.

The brown ring got bigger, and sudden-like, the top page just curled up, turned black, and crumbled to ash. Then the one under that. Quicker now, the one under that and the one under that, each one faster'n the one ahead of it, the one under that and the one under that, till that whole satanic book just flared up and died.

The End.

I felt like some terrible story had just finished, or maybe a war was over, something bad was done, and...

And I was wrong.

If the GraveWalker thing was mad before, he went plumb berserk now. Dashou raced away, dodging through the crowd, and that monster come after him, not through the crowd but plain damn overtop it, batting down anyone didn't get out of his way quick enough, and stepping on them that fell in the wrong direction. I emptied the Spencer on it, and maybe that slowed it up some, but far as I could tell, it was just a waste of time when there wasn't any time to waste, 'cause that beast was sure enough going to catch up with Dashou and when he did, he'd...

Just starting to think of it reminded me about the Baby. I swung down off the choir loft and made ready to fight through the crowd, like everybody else seemed to of done today, but that monster had made the job simple. Them as weren't burned, injured or trampled had lost interest when they saw this thing they'd conjured up turn on 'em. I made my way up to the table with the manger on it, and that infant was asleep or else passed out from breathing burning air. Either way, it needed getting away from here, and it looked like I could tote the manger out pretty easy now that Dashou had the GraveWalker all to himself. I looked around for the closest door...

...and saw Slasher Jim Trask's cutlass on the floor.

What come next I couldn't believe, but it sounded just like a voice come down to me—a voice from above, talking to me—talking to *me*, a fella who calls the Devil by his first name!

But I'd swear a voice come down, and it said to me,

Streak, it said, *pick up the sword and cut that sunuvabitch clear in two.*

And when I picked it up, I felt something, some surge maybe, run up my arm, and I turned around and hollered, "Dashou! Just you let that critter chase you up thisaway!"

I hunkered down behind the altar and listened for the noise of running feet, and as soon as Dashou raced past I jumped out holding the cutlass up and that damnable thing run himself right into it. Deep.

CHAPTER 49

The GraveWalker didn't stop there. Nothing that big moving that fast is going to stop for anything less than a rock wall, and right then the only rocks was in my head. It kept moving from sheer momentum, knocked me half-down, and raised up its hands towards my throat. I backed away fast, but kept hold of that cutlass, which was mostly still inside that awful critter.

And it wouldn't come loose!

I twisted and turned it as I pulled, and the thing let out a howl that was pure ungodly, raised its arms up over its head and just stared upwards for a long time—seemed so to me, anyhow— stared up like it saw something up above it never seen before. It clawed its fingers, like to grab whatever it was …

Then its knees went out and it fell all over me.

The weight of it like to crushed the air from my lungs, and for a time—I don't know how long—I was clear out. Then the weight seemed to shift. I come to and felt something moving over my body, warm and wet, oozing down …

It was bleeding all over me!

I looked up and it wasn't just *It* anymore; it was two things now, two things that had been men, years ago, and tried to be men again, but I'd stuck my foot in that idea.

"So they're properly dead now, and I collected two souls that thought they could dodge me for as long as ... Well, I guess they thought they never would have to pay the toll. Much obliged, Streak."

"Being obliged ain't your style, Harvey."

"How's that?"

"It ain't like you to go around owing me a favor."

He scratched his head over that one. "I guess you're right, young friend. What can I do for you? Fortune? Love? Money or power? Just name it, Pardner."

"How about you get these dead things off me before I choke to death in here, then help me get that baby-child outside before it does likeways?"

CHAPTER 50

Some time after all the dust and smoke settled, I got to thinking it over, what I'd done, and what happened, and what it meant—if it meant anything at all. There was something else bothered me too, so a day or so beyond all that fire and sword business, I met with the Devil to talk it all out.

"I mean, this Hinchley fella, he saved my life when I was a green kid in a grey uniform. Then just recent, he'd went to some pains to get me killed."

"And you paid him back by killing him first."

"Seems ungrateful on me, but that thing he turned into... "

"Quite a sight, wasn't it?" Harvey was by way of celebrating with a cigar while we took our ease in the saloon where all this started.

"Plenty bad enough to suit me, thank you."

"That Chinese fella sure took out after him, though, didn't he? He'll have a fine story to tell his kids when he gets back home."

"He can't go back." I shook my head. "Not ever. On account of he let that Hinchley and Trask kick those bones apart."

"Hold on there, Hoss. It was him helped you kill 'em."

"I'd of looked mighty puny trying to do it without him, and that's a fact. But from what I could piece together from his talk, he was supposed to be in charge of shipping them remains back to their family graveyards, or whatever, and he figures he didn't make a very tall job of it. Says he can't face the folks at home no more."

Harvey sighed and looked thoughtful. "Yeah, I guess Chinese are like that. Set a lot of store by their faces."

"Got me to thinking."

"Must be serious."

"No joking 'bout it." I mulled for a mite longer, then came out with it. "You still of a mind to do a deal? With me?"

"My arms are always open…"

"Yeah, for the poor sinner. I remember you saying that."

"Then state your terms, friend."

"Reckon I'll get me a drink first."

"Fine with me." He signaled the bartender. "But just one. I won't do business with a man who's muddy-headed."

The bartender poured him a shot of something, I didn't mind what, and pushed me a bottle of near-beer. When he was gone, Harvey passed me his drink and I downed it quick. I'm no stranger to hard liquor, but I don't go there much. This one warmed my insides and got me ready for what I wanted to say.

"Just tell me where she's gone."

"That Sally Gal?"

"You think I meant somebody else?"

"Just want to get it all clearly understood. You're ready to sell your soul just to see that lady again?"

"I said it, didn't I?"

"What if she scares you away? Word is, her face got bad cut up, you know."

"I ain't forgot that."

"And what if she won't have you?"

"'I'll take the chance. Got to."

"Streak," He sounded like a man being careful how to say something that ain't welcome to hear. "How's it you're so ready just now? It's almost two years since that business about you and the Appleys..."

"It ain't nothing to do with Appleys. It was that man from China. The way he talked about how he can't go back." I toyed with my empty shot glass. "He's got him a wife back home, a child he ain't seen in donkey's years, and won't ever see again. Won't see neither one of 'em."

"He said all that? Didn't strike me as the loquacious sort."

"I wondered on that myself. This jasper shows up at the Fargo office, looking to find me, only I don't work there no more. So he takes the trouble to track me, and shows up at the livery and starts telling me his sad story."

"Crying on your shoulder."

"I thought so at first, but like you say, he ain't a chin-waggin' man. I couldn't figure it myself, not sure for certain how long I stood there, trying to squeeze the sense out of the words he was saying—well you know how he talks."

"Uses the wrong words, and mispronounces the right ones."

"And then it come to me. He wasn't looking for pity." I searched some to put the right words to it. "He was warning me."

Harvey put a questioning look on his face and I obliged him.

"Dashou can't go back. Never gonna see the ones he loves. Wasn't his fault, but now he can't roll back home again.

"*I can.*

"He was telling me that. I can go back, maybe. Leastways, I got a chance—if I take it. He don't have a chance, and maybe I won't always have one neither. So I guess I better get to it."

I looked down at the empty shot glass, then back up at Harvey.

"That's it. Just point me where to find Sally Gal, and when time comes… How long till you take my soul, anyhow?"

He slid my empty shot glass back over in front of him. Somewhere along the way, it filled up again. "Right now I'm likely as close to taking your soul as I'll ever get." He raised his glass in a one-man toast to me and tossed it off in one swallow.

"I told you one time I don't take a man's soul for doing a good deed. It's frowned on in the circles I frequent, and I'd be snubbed in polite society."

I knew he was kidding around, but I wasn't in no mood for it.

"You going to tell me what I'm asking, or not?"

"I'm going to do that very thing, Streak. And it ain't going to cost you any part of your soul at all."

"If you mean another deal like the last one…"

"Don't go throwing a man's past misdeeds in his face."

"Why not?"

"Because I invented it, and I make a pretty good living at it, so I don't need the competition." There was joking in how he said it, but something maybe a little sad, too. "The fact is, I still owe you for the two souls you sent me. Hinchley and Trask, you know. And I always aim to part on the square."

"We're parting?"

"Pretty soon now. They say *'If you don't succeed, try again. Then give up.'* no sense being a damn fool, you know. And Streak, I'm giving up on you."

"Harvey, sometimes I don't understand you. And now is one of 'em."

"Two years ago, you'd have been a real prize. The Best Shot in Ware County. If word got out that you sold your soul to the Devil, it woulda raised my stock thereabouts considerable." He came out with a sigh. "But you ain't in Ware County anymore. Come to that, Ware County doesn't amount to as much as it did. Once I measure up your lack of prestige against the social stigma of taking your soul for doing good, I just don't see any profit by it."

"So what you're saying is—"

"What I'm saying is she's got her another place. It ain't much, but she makes a living at it. And where it's at ain't much, either. Little crossroads place by Stinking Creek. Folks there call it Hogshead Corners."

"Harvey, I'm obliged."

"No you're not. Fact is, you don't owe me a thing. And I don't owe you anything either."

I considered on that some. "You're a square dealer. I'll miss your company."

"And I'll miss yours. So I'll tell you this--"

His voice got real serious, and he looked at me straight on. "—If you ever want something personal for yourself. Something pure selfish, just for you ..." He stepped away from the bar and put on his hat. "Just mention my name. Usual rates apply."

CHAPTER 51

Hogshead Corners was two days' ride and then some. Time I got there I was ripe as a stepped-on melon, but they had a place a man could get a shave and a bath, just off the livery stable—I come to find out the barber helped out at the livery when hair-scalping business was slow, which was mostly--so I got me freshened up decent, and whilst I was getting dressed I asked was there a place to get a drink thereabouts.

"Just the one, Scarface Sal's." The barber shucked off his white jacket, and the place filled up with stable-smell from his dirt-worn dungarees and straw-flecked shirt. "But it's good enough for the hands—farmhands and cowhands I mean— they fill it up come Saturday, and she keeps cots for them as need sleeping it off."

But I'd quit listening after "Scarface Sal."

Sally Gal's place back in Gunder's Station wasn't big nor fancy, but this place wasn't much more'n half the size. It was clean, though. Well-kept and, hard to say exactly, it just looked comfortable and cared about.

There was no one behind the bar when I came in, but right away a woman came out through a curtain that separated the front from the back. The sun was just in the right place to stream light through the window and hit her head-on, showing every line in her face.

She hadn't changed.

Same face I fell in love with two years back. At my age, two years is a good chunk of your life, but she looked just the same.

She stepped behind the bar, and closer-up I could maybe see another line or two on her face, and if I looked hard enough... yeah, there was a long scar down one side, close to her hairline, and along her chin. So faint I couldn't see it hardly at all.

She came up smiling with the patient, paid-for smile of every bartender everywhere, and the way she said "Howdy, stranger," was as friendly as warm sunshine—and just about as personal.

Then I realized the sun that was on her face was keeping mine in shadow. I moved so's the light hit me and said, "Hello, Sally Gal."

She looked at me.

For the longest time in my life, she just looked at me, and I tried to read the feelings behind her eyes.

Finally, she said, "You've changed."

"Not you," I said. She saw my face and knew I meant it.

"You're crazy."

"Never had a clearer thought in my head than coming here. Nor a better one."

There was a long quiet between us. Then somehow it got to be a comfortable silence, like between two old married folks.

"Well," Sally Gal said at last, "What brings you here?"

"I'm thinking you know what."

"And I think you made a long trip for nothing."

There was something in her voice told me it hurt her to say that. And that same something, whatever it was, also said she'd carved it in stone.

Her eyes softened as she spoke. "Yes, I loved you once, but loving you was a mistake, and I don't love you now, and I won't love you again, and there's nothing you can say or do to change that."

Funny. I got to thinking then about my smashed tombstone. And about Pug Klavinsky. How he kept telling us and telling us over again that he never killed our Fargo driver. And all the time, there was nothing he could say to change our minds. He knew that, and we knew it, but he just kept talking and wasting his last breath.

I was in those shoes now. Dying standing up, just like that no-account back-shooter.

It wasn't going to happen with us. Not because of anything I said or did. Because of what I *was*. Because of what I *am*.

Which was wrong for Sally Gal.

So I gave up, No sense being a damn fool about it.

Two cowboys came in to wet the dust, and that was my cue to turn and leave. Would have liked to say some special kind of Goodbye. Would have liked to got a hug, or a kiss, maybe, but there was nothing like that. And if they made any words for what I was feeling, I sure hadn't come across them.

So there was nothing special about how I took my leave. Just me walking out the door.

CHAPTER 52

Outside, the sun had set, and the stars just starting to come out.

"Harvey?" I said. "You there?"